STING

of the

BLUE SCORPION

The
STING
of the
BLUE SCORPION

*To Bob
From Russ*

RUSSELL PELTON

outskirtspress
DENVER, COLORADO

The Sting of the Blue Scorpion
All Rights Reserved.
Copyright © 2016 Russell Pelton
v1.0

Outskirts Press, Inc.
http://www.outskirtspress.com

ISBN: 978-1-4787-6686-5

Outskirts Press and the "OP" logo are trademarks belonging to Outskirts Press, Inc.

PRINTED IN THE UNITED STATES OF AMERICA

Disclaimer

This is a work of fiction. Any resemblance of persons, places or events depicted in this novel to any actual persons, places or events is entirely coincidental, except for the fact that Wurtsmith Air Force Base in Oscoda, Michigan was the home of SAC's 379th Bombardment Wing during the 1960's.

This book is dedicated to the thousands of attorneys who, over the years, have served as Judge Advocates in the United States military, whether serving all or a significant portion of their professional careers as JAG officers, and often facing moral/ethical dilemmas similar to those raised in this novel.

Acknowledgement is made of the invaluable contributions to the production of my novels by Glenda Kovac, my assistant for twenty-five years.

Chapter 1

—*mm*—

Peggy Wilton would have seen the man standing in the shadows if it hadn't been so cold.

She walked out the side door of the Officers' Club, pulled her parka hood over her head, and turned her face away from the icy wind blowing in off Lake Huron. Few people had ventured out in the sub-zero Michigan weather that night. The dining room normally closed at ten but tonight all the waitresses, including Peggy, were let off an hour early.

It was early January at Wurtsmith Air Force Base. Winter's deep chill had set in, and the Straits of Mackinac, one hundred and fifty miles to the northwest, had frozen over. Many of the local residents, those not tied to the base, had long ago fled to the south, and the few who remained were clustered in the neighboring town of Oscoda. Peggy's parents, who farmed land to the north, had gone to Florida for their annual vacation, and were coming back soon. Before they left Peggy thought it would be cool to have the whole house to herself. Now she wished she had gone with them.

The cold blue light of the full moon showed Peggy the path to the rear section of the Club's parking lot, where her Impala was half buried in the snow. She dreaded the thought of having to dig it out, but was grateful that her father had insisted that she use studded tires. Those would help. A pickup truck with a camper was parked alongside the path between her and her Impala, but the lot was otherwise empty.

She dug her gloved hands deep into the parka's fur-lined pockets and hunched her shoulders in a futile attempt to gain a little more warmth. Her boots made a staccato crunching sound as she walked over the path's frozen snow toward her car. The only other sound was the distant hum of the generators on the flight line.

Behind her, a tall hooded figure stepped out of the shadows and began following her down the path. He matched her step for step, and his longer stride slowly closed the gap between them. The parka pulled over her ears muffled his approach. As she neared the pickup truck he bolted forward. He grabbed her, spun her around and slammed his fist into her face. He caught her with one hand before she could fall, and with the other hand grabbed the camper's door handle and flung it open. He threw her in the rear, jumped in after her, and yanked the door shut.

An enclosed jeep bounced along the perimeter road on the north side of the base. The two air policemen inside were conducting their daily check of the base's outer fence. The morning air was bitter cold.

To the right, off the road, twenty yards beyond the fence, a wall of towering pines stood like a fortress. To the left, a sea of the whitest snow swept to the distant runway, undulating only occasionally to mark shrubs and bushes buried beneath.

Suddenly, the jeep skidded to a halt. The driver shifted into neutral, rolled down his window, and said, nodding to his left, "Something's over there, Sarge. Something dark. Wasn't there yesterday."

"Better check it out. I'll wait here."

Airman Bill Pollard grunted, pushed his door open, and stepped out of the jeep. He pulled his parka hood forward, and left the road to wade through the deep snow to the spot where he had seen something.

"Jesus Christ, Sarge," he shouted. "Look at this!"

Staff Sergeant Mike Dahlke got out and trudged through the drifts toward Airman Pollard. When he reached his side, he saw her. The body of a blond young woman was lying face up in a shallow depression. She was nude from the waist down and her thighs were smeared with blood. Her head was pulled back and was surrounded by crimson ice. Her throat had been slit.

3

"Mayor Schroeder to see you, sir."

Carl Schroeder pushed aside the airman and stormed into the office of the man in charge at Wurtsmith Air Force Base, Wing Commander, Colonel Alex Breckenridge. The Mayor was a big man, and his thick-soled arctic boots, his heavy duty overcoat (its hood still covering his head), and the scowl on his weather-beaten face, rendered him quite imposing. He was livid with anger.

Colonel Breckenridge quickly rose and walked around his large mahogany desk. "This is a terrible thing that's happened, Carl," he said as he extended his hand. "Do you know the girl's family?"

"*Know* them?" The white-haired mayor shouted, his face twisted in rage, ignoring Breckenridge's extended hand. "Charlie Wilton is one of my best friends. He's the president of the School Board. Millie and I were at Peggy's baptism, for God's sake. Yeah, I know them!"

"I'm sorry. I should have realized that, here in Oscoda." He turned to the airman who still stood in the doorway looking embarrassed. "Take the mayor's coat and bring us both some coffee - strong. And Bill, ask Major Davis to join us."

Colonel Breckenridge gestured to the leather couch as the young man left the room. "Have a seat, Carl. And try to stay calm."

"Don't patronize me, Alex!" Mayor Schroeder growled as he sat down slowly, his eyes never leaving Breckenridge. "One of your men killed her. We both know that. I want that bastard found!"

4

Alex Breckenridge had been in the military for twenty-six years. He was a bomber pilot in World War II, and joined the Strategic Air Command when Curtis LeMay took command of it in 1948. He became a major and a command pilot during Korea. Now in his late forties he'd become stockier and began to resemble his idol, LeMay. Breckenridge enjoyed the likeness, and fostered it by chain-smoking long, dark Panamil cigars. SAC gave him the Wurtsmith command in 1965 to see if he could fly a desk as well as he could fly a bomber. At first he was disappointed, fearing Wurtsmith was a dead end. Now, however, with the Cold War heating up and an escalating conflict in Viet Nam, as commander of one of America's most important military units, loaded with lethal weapons, he had a different view of its possibilities.

Wurtsmith was the home of SAC's 379th Bombardment Wing. Unlike many other military installations, which were preoccupied with training, supply, and public relation functions as well as the appeasement of local congressmen, Wurtsmith had an uncomplicated and highly focused mission. If a war began, Wurtsmith's thirty-six B-52's were to deliver H-bombs and Armageddon to seventy-two preselected Soviet cities and military bases, each of which was double-targeted to ensure its oblivion. Each plane also had two Hound Dog missiles carrying nuclear weapons slung under its wings to shoot its way through any air defenses they encountered as they entered Soviet air space, although it was expected that the waves of Titan missiles soaring above and ahead of them would destroy most of those Russian resources before the armada of bombers arrived.

Like most of the other twenty SAC bases with similar missions, Wurtsmith had been intentionally built in a remote northern location to minimize the time needed for its bombers to reach their Russian targets.

1968 had just begun. Alex Breckenridge knew that his command at Wurtsmith was under evaluation. Within six months he would either earn a star and move to SAC Headquarters in Omaha, or slip quietly into the Air Force's backwaters. The fact that he was commander of a front-line attack wing meant that any accomplishments or flaws in his command would be highly scrutinized. The last thing he needed right now was a local scandal or an unsolved murder under his command.

"Carl, you know my executive officer, Major Davis, don't you?" Breckenridge asked as the door opened and a tall, thin officer in his mid-thirties stepped in.

"James Lee Davis, Mr. Mayor," the younger man said along with a firm handshake. "I believe we met last summer at the Chamber of Commerce golf outing." His voice carried a trace of a Virginia drawl.

"Yes, I recall," Schroeder replied curtly.

Major Davis pulled up an armchair and sat down facing the other two men. He was impeccably dressed in a blue Air Force uniform that had been tailored for him by Brooks Brothers. At six-foot one he had steel blue eyes, blond hair and a thin mustache.

Colonel Breckenridge's orderly returned with a pot of coffee, poured it into three china cups and left the room.

The wing commander took a sip, and looked up at Davis.

"Jimmy, we were just discussing this murder that occurred last night. Terrible thing. Carl is convinced that one of our men did it."

"He's probably right," Davis replied coolly. "After all, three-quarters of the men around here this time of year are Air Force personnel. If you add to that the fact that the killing occurred on base, you're probably running the odds up to over ninety percent that he's one of ours. Sorry, Colonel, but that's a fact of life we've got to live with."

"Well, goddamn it then," the Mayor huffed, slamming his fist on the adjacent coffee table and rattling the china. "It's your responsibility to find that bastard." His eyes snapped from Breckenridge to Davis. "We've never had a murder in Oscoda before. Ever!" he thundered. "And Peggy Wilton, of all people." He shook his head in disbelief.

Major Davis began to say something, but Carl Schroeder cut him off.

"And let me tell you something else," he said, leaning forward. "When you find that son-of-a-bitch, there are a lot of people around here who'd be willing to bet any amount of money he's one of your Negroes. You and I know that's not necessarily the case, but you've been bringing more and more of *them* in here, and they're taking over the whole damn town. That's not what some people had in mind when they invited the Air Force here in the first place. I've had nightmares that something like this would happen, the way some of the folks fear, and now it's come true. I'm sick. Just sick."

"Carl, don't jump to any conclusions," Colonel Breckenridge answered. "At this point it could be anybody. But I'll tell you this. If Jimmy Davis here is right and that killer is one of ours, we'll find him and we'll convict him. You've got my word on that."

He turned to Major Davis, "Jimmy, call the Office of Special Investigations at SAC Headquarters, explain the situation to them, and tell them that it's my personal request that Mitch Pawlowski take charge of this case. I'd like him to be the investigating officer. He's the best Special Agent they've got and he's stationed right here. This should be number one on the OSI's priority list, as well as ours, until the killer is nailed. Do you understand?"

"Yes, sir. I'll do it right now," Davis said as he rose. "Mr. Mayor, I'll keep you updated daily on the progress of our investigation."

"Thank you, I'd appreciate that," Schroeder replied.

Davis nodded, turned and left the room.

When the door clicked shut, Carl Schroeder put his coffee cup down, stared at it for a moment, then looked up at the wing commander. "Alex, let me ask you something," he said. "You still have capital punishment in the military, don't you?"

"We sure do. And you can bet your ass that murder and aggravated rape are capital offenses in our book."

"Fine. I'm going to tell the Sheriff to defer to the military on this investigation. I want your guys to find this bastard. And when you find him, I want him tried in a military court. I'll waive civil jurisdiction; our stupid Governor has blocked every potential execution we've had for the last five years. I want this son-of-a-bitch to burn!"

"We use the firing squad in the Air Force, Carl, but you can count on that."

Later that afternoon, an old two-door tan Ford pulled up to Wurtsmith's front gate maneuvering its way through a small crowd of anti-war protestors. It was spattered with a grimy mixture of mud, ice and road salt. The young couple in the front seat were apprehensive as a helmeted air policeman wearing mirrored sunglasses and a short but heavy jacket approached their car. A holstered .45 hung at his side below the jacket. Behind him two other airmen stood watching from a small concrete building; one controlling the lowered metal gate; the other keeping his automatic rifle leveled at the dozen or so protestors shouting at them, fifty feet away.

Tony and Karen Jeffries had driven that day from Chicago, all their possessions loaded into the old Ford. An ironing board, which Karen's mother had insisted they take, rested atop a pile of clothes, boxes and lamps in the back seat, butting up against the right rear window.

It had been an exhausting seven-hour drive, the last three hours through non-stop snow. Tony turned off the radio, interrupting the Beatles' "Hey Jude," which they had heard at least twenty times that day on their long drive from Chicago. They were both excited about getting to Wurtsmith Air Force Base. This would be Tony's first real job since passing the Illinois bar exam. DePauw's ROTC program had committed Tony to three years in the Air Force, and he was glad to avoid being drafted and have his military obligation deferred while he attended the University of Chicago Law School. His time in the military wasn't going to be wasted. He'd be practicing law, learning his profession.

Tony rolled down his window and was suddenly blinded by the ice crystals that blew past his wire rim glasses into his eyes.

"Can I help you?" he heard.

"Yes, you can," Tony said, removing his glasses and wiping the cold moisture from his cheek. "I'm reporting for duty with the Base Legal Office."

"May I see your orders, please," the air policeman asked crisply.

"Sure." Tony turned and began thumbing through the assorted papers and maps next to him on the front seat. Without his glasses it was hard for him to tell one document from another.

"Here they are," Karen said, pulling some stapled white pages from the pile and handing them to Tony. He gave the orders to the air policeman, then cleaned off his glasses with a handkerchief he pulled from a pocket.

The airman checked Tony's papers, looked inside the

car, nodded to Karen and asked "May I see your identification, ma'am."

"Sure" Karen said, with a smile as she handed him her Illinois driver's license, which he quickly reviewed, comparing its photo with the woman in the car, returned her license, then stepped back and saluted.

"Welcome to Wurtsmith Air Force Base, Lieutenant Jeffries. I suggest you check into the Temporary Housing Office first. That's in building A-100, about a half mile ahead on the right. The Legal Office is in the Base Headquarters Building, across the street from it."

"Thank you." Tony saluted back and smiled. He felt silly saluting in jeans and an old Bears sweatshirt. He looked like anything but an Air Force officer.

"You're going to have to get used to that," Karen laughed as they drove through the gate. "I think you're in the Army now."

"The Air Force, Karen. The Air Force."

Dusk was falling as they drove up the long main drive of the base. That combined with the steadily falling snow, made it hard to see too far ahead. All the vehicles they passed had their headlights on, and Tony defensively turned his on too. They hadn't seen this much activity in the last two hours of their drive.

There was a stop sign at the first intersection they came to, and they waited as a dozen men crossed the road in front of them. All were dressed in thickly padded light green parkas with strips of reflector tape on the arms and backs. Very little flesh was exposed to the weather.

"Everyone looks so serious, Tony."

"I know. I wonder what they do for entertainment here. It's so bleak."

They passed rows of low wooden buildings on both sides. In the distance, slowly emerging from the swirling clouds of snow, a collection of much larger buildings took shape. As they got closer, Tony realized that they were hangars, and in front of each was a huge gray plane. These were the B-52's. Teams of armed men with guard dogs roamed the area around them.

A second chain-link fence blocked the road to the flight line. Tony was so fascinated with the scene in front of him that he almost ran into the gate. When he stopped, he found that they were immediately in front of building A-100, an undistinguished two-story wooden structure.

He pulled into the plowed parking lot beside the building, and they both went in.

The airman in the Temporary Housing Office assigned Tony and Karen apartment 24, on the building's second floor. It was the only vacant unit, he explained, and it was free only because Lieutenant Nagy and his family left for Saigon a week ago. It had two bedrooms and some basic furniture, he said, and would be their quarters until one of the officers' houses opened up which might take three or four months.

Apartment 24 was at the top of the stairs at one end of a short hallway that appeared to lead to three other units. The smell of fresh paint was in the air as Tony and Karen struggled to open the door, each of them carrying an armload of hanging clothes and dragging a suitcase. Tony fumbled with the key before the lock finally turned, pushed the door open and stepped inside. Karen found the light switch to her right, and turned it on with her elbow.

"Tony, this is beautiful." Karen said with a smile as she walked in and looked around.

The combination living-dining room was furnished simply, but adequately. On one end was an upholstered couch, two upholstered chairs, an Admiral fourteen-inch TV set on a black metal stand and a coffee table; a small dining table with four cane-backed chairs at the other, adjacent to the kitchen.

There were windows on both sides; to the east, they could see in the late afternoon dusk through a momentary break in the snow, the distant trees, rooftops and chimneys of Oscoda, and beyond them, the glistening gray waters of Lake Huron.

"Not too bad," Tony said as he walked toward the bedrooms in back. He glanced at Karen. "You know," he said, "this is bigger than the apartment we had in Hyde Park."

Karen laughed, "What are we ever going to do with a whole house when we get one?"

"Beats me," Tony said, dumping his armload of clothes on the double bed in the larger bedroom. "Tell you what; if you want to start sorting this out, I'll bring up the rest of the stuff from the car."

"That's a great deal. I accept." Karen laid some of the clothes she was carrying on the bed, and took the rest over to the closet. She looked as grungy as Tony, wearing old jeans and a faded Cubs sweatshirt, unkempt hair and no make-up.

"I knew it," she laughed when she opened the closet door. An ironing board was leaning up against the wall.

Within twenty minutes Tony had brought up the rest of their belongings. He showered, shaved and put on his Air Force uniform. He'd been told to report to the Legal Office as soon as he arrived, but he didn't want to look like a street person when he did.

"I shouldn't be too long." he told Karen. "When I get back we'll find someplace for a nice dinner."

Tony's biggest problem as he entered the Headquarters Building was not finding the Legal Office, but figuring out who to salute first, and who to salute only after they saluted him. He solved the problem by saluting everyone in uniform as he walked down the corridor. All of them returned his salute, but some did so with a curious smile.

The Legal Office was in the east wing of the building. Tony introduced himself to the receptionist, a thin woman in her fifties in a thick blue sweater, her graying auburn hair pulled back in a bun. She rose and shook his hand. "Welcome to Wurtsmith, Lieutenant. I'm Ruth Olmsted. Let me take you back to meet Lieutenant Colonel Goldsmith," she said with a smile. "He's been waiting for you."

She led Tony a few yards down a carpeted hallway, walking with short, crisp steps that reminded him of his fourth grade teacher, Mrs. Horning. They stopped at a

14

wooden door with "Staff Judge Advocate" painted on it. She knocked once; and pushed it open a crack.

"Colonel Goldsmith, Lieutenant Jeffries is here."

"Fine. Send him on in," Tony heard a friendly voice answer.

Ruth Olmsted turned to Tony, smiled, and waved him in.

"Hello, Jeffries. Good to meet you." Mel Goldsmith smiled as he rose from his desk and took Tony's hand. He was a small man, no more than five-six and balding with thin wisps of hair carefully combed across the top of his head. He was in his mid-forties, Tony guessed. A cigarette dangled from his left hand and his accent was distinctly New Yawk. His shirt collar unbuttoned and his tie loosened, he looked much more like a working lawyer than an Air Force career officer. He seemed genuinely pleased to see Tony.

They made small talk for a few minutes, and Goldsmith said he'd like to show Tony around the office. "It's not much," he said with a chuckle, "but it's the biggest law office in Iosco County." He didn't add that there were just two other lawyers in the county, one of them semi-retired.

Walking down the corridor, Goldsmith pointed out the conference room and their small law library. The walls were all painted a medium brown, which went well with the beige carpeting. The clickety-clack of a typewriter, punctuated regularly by its bell, drifted from somewhere down the hall. "The next office," Goldsmith said, "is Major Cunningham's."

"Bob's the next senior man here," Goldsmith said, "after me." The door was ajar, but he knocked on it once and pushed it fully open. "You're going to like working with him."

Inside was a tall black man in his mid-thirties, with a strong chin and high cheek bones. He looked at Tony for a moment, smiling and said, "You must be Jeffries. It's about time you got here! We've got a ton of work for you." He laughed as he gripped Tony's hand and shook it firmly.

"My pleasure," Tony said after a brief pause. He hadn't anticipated that he'd be working for a black man; there'd only been a handful of black students in his law school class.

Turning to Goldsmith, Cunningham said, "Mel, we've finally got someone new to give all the junk work and sonic boom claims. My life has just improved one hundred percent."

"Do you mean that there are only..." Tony's voice trailed off as he looked at the major.

"That's right," Mel Goldsmith answered with a smile. "There are only three of us. So you're going to have plenty to do."

"Before you panic," Cunningham added, "we do have another lieutenant reporting next week. That'll bring us up to full strength. You'll have the vacant office next to mine." The office was small and stark, but it was Tony's own and he was excited. He could see his law books filling the empty bookcase and his license proudly hanging on the wall behind the metal desk.

Tony liked these men and looked forward to working with them. It struck him that Bob Cunningham must be very sharp indeed to be a major. He also knew that for the first year or so he'd be handling the office's most routine matters, and shouldn't expect to get involved in anything really substantial. But what did he care? He was a working lawyer now!

Chapter 2

—*mm*—

Mitch Pawlowski went over Peggy Wilton's autopsy again. He had probably read it a hundred times in the week since she was killed. He was sitting in his office in the OSI section of the Headquarters Building, photos and reports from the Wilton case covering his desk.

According to the autopsy she had died of severe blood loss resulting from slashed carotid arteries on both sides of her neck. He judged that her death was swift once her throat was cut, but she must have suffered a great deal before that. She had a fractured right cheekbone and a broken nose. Those must have been her first injuries, Pawlowski concluded, because some of the blood from those wounds had been washed away by tears. Peggy seemed to have cried a lot in the process of dying.

There were two cracked ribs on her lower left side, and her right ankle was broken, the autopsy read. That probably happened when the bastard tore her boots off, Pawlowski thought. He hadn't cared how much pain he was causing her. Or worse, maybe the pain was the point.

And, of course, she was raped. Brutally, causing lacerations and tearings, both external and internal. The Iosco County Medical Examiner concluded from his analysis of her bruises that she had been raped twice: once before she died, once afterwards.

We're looking for one sick son-of-a-bitch, Pawlowski said to himself as he laid the autopsy aside. *Brutal and sick.*

Mitch Pawlowski had been a cop all his adult life. He'd grown up in Cleveland, graduated from Ohio State, and enlisted in the Army Air Force in 1942. He'd become an M.P., and after the war he got a job with the Cleveland Police Department. When he was recalled to service during the Korean War, he decided to stay. He was assigned to the Office of Special Investigations, the Air Force's elite investigative branch, and for the past two years he'd headed the OSI office at Wurtsmith.

As an OSI agent, Pawlowski wore civilian clothes with a Smith & Wesson .38 in a shoulder holster. In the shadow world of criminal investigation, he found it more comfortable to operate with a civilian's relative autonomy. Everyone addressed him as "Mr. Pawlowski" or "Mitch". Only a handful of men at Wurtsmith knew he was a major.

He was expecting a call from Colonel Breckenridge or his exec, Jimmy Davis. One or the other had called him every day since the Wilton murder, demanding an update on his investigation. He thumbed through the papers on his desk and found a penciled note. As of noon that day his men had interviewed 167 people. None of those interviews had resulted in a single lead. That was all that Pawlowski could tell Breckenridge or Davis when they called. He picked up the autopsy report again. There *had* to be something there.

His concentration was broken when a young airman burst into his office. "Mitch, we've got a lead in the Wilton case," he said breathlessly.

"What did you find?" Pawlowski answered, quickly standing.

"Two eyewitnesses. A young couple who were parked on the far side of the runway. In the woods, down at the end. Probably necking. They saw a pickup truck coming down the back road from the Officers' Club about nine-thirty that night. And they saw the driver."

"Great!" Pawlowski said as he stepped around his desk, moving quickly toward the door. "And they're here?"

"Down the hall. In room 3."

—*mm*—

Tony and Karen Jeffries were settling into Wurtsmith, and enjoying it. They found that the Base Exchange had everything they needed, from linens and towels to food and kitchen supplies, all sales tax free. That helped since the Jeffries had only three hundred dollars between them when they arrived, and were down to seventy dollars by the end of the first week. They were being very careful with their expenses. But they loved it all the same. They enjoyed setting up their own home after living for two years in married student housing in Chicago.

They'd both grown up in the Chicago suburb of Riverside, and began dating at DePauw University, where Karen was a Tri-Delt and Tony, a year older, was a Lambda Chi. Their frat and sorority houses were right across the street from each other. They developed a very close and comfortable relationship in college, and by the time Tony graduated in 1964 they'd decided to partner in whatever adventures lay ahead.

Tony became interested in debate at DePauw, and did well at it. He enjoyed thinking on his feet and won a number of tournaments his junior and senior years. He loved the competition. He'd been a track and cross-country runner in high school, but not a star. In debate, he found for the first time a field in which he could compete, and win, regularly. Law school seemed a logical next step and he luckily made the cut at his first choice, the University of Chicago.

The Air Force was the only arm of the military with a ROTC program at DePauw. Tony enrolled in order to avoid the draft when he graduated, and to have some control over when he would have to serve. All young men owed the military three-years of service, and it was easily preferable to spend that time as an officer. He was commissioned a second lieutenant the day he graduated from DePauw and placed on inactive reserve. His three years of active duty were deferred while he attended law school.

Tony was surprised that his first assignment was Wurtsmith, an operational SAC base. He had received an automatic promotion to first lieutenant while in the reserves in law school. As a result, he was viewed by the personnel that make assignment decisions as being not only a lawyer, but an experienced one. In fact, when he arrived at Wurtsmith, Tony Jeffries had never even seen a real trial.

He spent all his free time that first week reading the Uniform Code of Military Justice, and everything related to it that he could find.

—*mm*—

Colonel Alex Breckenridge was sipping Jack Daniels in his office with his deputy, Jimmy Lee Davis, at six that evening. They often finished the day that way, before retiring to the Officers' Club for more formal drinking.

The wing commander's office had pine-paneled walls and the same beige carpeting found throughout the Headquarters Building. It was easily the best furnished office on base. Colonel Breckenridge's mahogany desk was flanked by furled flags of the United States and the Strategic Air Command. Behind the desk were a credenza and a view looking down Wurtsmith's two-mile flood-lit main runway. A couch and a half-dozen pull-up chairs, all in brown leather, filled out the room.

Even though Breckenridge was older than Davis and more senior in rank, the two shared many interests and friends. Breckenridge had been raised in Charleston, South Carolina and attended the Citadel. Davis, whose father was a Navy admiral, spent most of his youth at Newport News, Virginia, and graduated from the Virginia Military Institute in Lexington. The annual VMI-Citadel game usually caused a fair amount of money to change hands between them.

The major was always careful, though, to maintain the proper respect for the wing commander. Davis was no fool, and he intended to come away from this assignment with an excellent rating and an early promotion to lieutenant Colonel.

This evening they weren't reminiscing about the Old South. They were talking about the murder. They both knew that the killer could very well be one of the twenty or so men they could see working in the hangar area, while they spoke.

"I don't like it, Jimmy," Breckenridge said, puffing on his cigar. "This whole investigation's moving too slowly. Mitch hasn't come up with a damn thing yet."

"I know," Davis replied. "Mayor Schroeder called twice today. I had to tell him that we didn't have anything to report. Both times. He's really getting pissed off."

"Damn!" Breckenridge looked past his deputy, down the long runway.

"Colonel, you've been out in West Texas, haven't you?" Davis asked after a moment. "The area out beyond

Odessa and our training bases?"

"I sure have, Jimmy. Real god-forsaken country. Why do you ask?"

"Well, it just struck me that the problem we've got right now is just like being in West Texas."

"How's that?" Breckenridge leaned forward and poured them both some more Jack Daniels.

"You can look out over that West Texas countryside, Colonel, and you can't see a single living thing. Nothing! But if you kick over one of those rocks on the ground, sometimes you'll find a bright red scorpion. He was there all the time, you just couldn't see him. And if you're not careful when you kick that rock over, he's going to sting you real good." Davis paused to take another sip of his whiskey. "That's what we've got here, Colonel. A killer we just can't see. He's out there, though, just like that scorpion. Waiting for the right rock to be turned over. We've just got to make damn sure he doesn't sting anyone else."

"A scorpion. Yes, I like that," Breckenridge said, half to himself. Looking at Davis, he touched his Air Force jacket and added, "But in this case, a blue scorpion."

A knock at the door interrupted their conversation.

"Come in," Breckenridge shouted.

The door swung open and Mitch Pawlowski stepped in. He had a tight smile on his face as his eyes danced from Breckenridge to Davis.

"Glad I found you, Colonel," he said approaching Breckenridge's desk. "I have something you might be interested in." He pulled a folded piece of paper from an inside jacket pocket and handed it to Breckenridge who reached up and took it, his eyes on the husky investigator.

"What in the hell is this?"

"It's a list of men, Colonel. One of them is your killer."

"How the hell do you know that, Mitch?" Breckenridge put down his cigar and stared at Pawlowski who had thrown his heavy coat over one of the chairs.

"We found a couple of witnesses; local teenagers. They saw a man driving away from the club the night of the murder. It was just the right time and place. He was driving a Ford pickup with a camper." Pawlowski paused, "And they're both sure he was a Negro."

"Damn! Well, that confirms that he's one of ours," Major Davis said, shaking his head. "There aren't any colored civilians in Iosco County."

"Hell, Mitch, even if that's true, that doesn't tell us much," Breckenridge said derisively. "We've got over a thousand Negro men on base."

"But only eight of them own Ford pickups with campers. I had one of my men check with Base Vehicle Registration. Just got the report. These are the eight." He pointed to the folded piece of paper in Breckenridge's hand as he sat down in one of the chairs on the other side of the desk, next to Davis.

"What about stolen cars?" Davis asked. "Were there any reports of stolen Ford pickups that night? Either on base or in the county?"

"None. We checked." Pawlowski nodded toward the

folded document. "One of those men is our killer. You can bank on that. We're in the process right now of interviewing them and examining all their vehicles."

Breckenridge quickly unfolded the paper. As he did, Major Davis rose from his chair, stepped over to the Colonel's side and looked down at the typed list. It was in alphabetical order:

> Airman 1st Class Joseph Banes
> Staff Sergeant Clarence Bowan
> Airman 2nd Class Robert Dawson
> Senior Master Sergeant Marcus Jackson
> Staff Sergeant DeWitt Nance
> 1st Lieutenant William Robbins
> Airman 2nd Class George Torrance
> Technical Sergeant Franklin Wallace

There was a long silence as both men studied the list. Finally, Davis spoke. "Well, it couldn't have been Lieutenant Robbins. He's been on leave in Detroit the past two weeks. I signed his orders myself."

"Did he take his pickup with him?" Pawlowski asked.

"I'm sure he did. It's his only vehicle. But we can verify that."

"If that's right, it cuts our list down to seven. Damn, this is good work, Mitch!" Breckenridge said approvingly. "Keep checking out the rest of those guys and see if there's anyone else we can cross off."

"I hope there is," Davis added. "When Mayor

Schroeder learns that the killer's a negro, he's going to go absolutely crazy. It's exactly what he was afraid of. If we don't arrest someone damn fast, he's going to bring in either the State Police or the FBI. Either way, we look bad."

"Jimmy's right, Mitch." Breckenridge nodded and paused to re-light his cigar. He slowly exhaled a cloud of smoke and looked up at Pawlowski. "I don't care how you do it," he said quietly. "But you've got to decide which one of those men did it, and get him arrested on the double. That's a goddamn order!"

———

The man took a deep swig of his Four Roses, leaned back, shut his eyes, and savored the sweetness trickling down his throat. He screwed the top back on the bottle, laid it on the seat beside him, and looked back at the building's side door. It was almost two a.m. and he had been waiting there for half an hour, parked deep in the shadows of the pine forest that surrounded the building. This was the time she usually came out. *Where is she?*

It wasn't long. Some of the lights went out, the door to the building opened, and she stepped out; her coat wasn't fully buttoned, and he could see her beautiful legs as she walked to her car. He could feel the excitement rising in him as he watched her every move, her hair blowing behind her in the light breeze off the lake. *Will this be the night? Yeah, probably.* He had been waiting and watching her too long. He wanted her tonight. *That white bitch needs some good fucking, just as much as I need to give it to her.*

Then someone else stepped out of the building; another woman, shorter and stockier. She got into the passenger's side of the car and shut the door. "Damn," he muttered. *This is no good, not at all. Not tonight, but soon. Soon,* he thought as the other car pulled out of the parking lot onto the main road, heading north. *Yes, soon!*

Chapter 3

By January twenty-second Mitch Pawlowski's men had cut the suspect list down to five. Airman Banes's pickup had been up on blocks since the end of October, and Sergeant Jackson's was in a body shop in Tawas City. Neither was operable the night of the murder.

The five remaining men were questioned at length. While all had alibis, none was firm enough to justify removing another name from the list. None had any apparent connection with Peggy Wilton, and the physical examination of the trucks and campers had been inconclusive. The killer evidently had the foresight to clean up after his butchery.

As Major Davis had predicted, Carl Schroeder became more and more outraged with every passing day. *That damn murdering piece of trash is still loose!* As Mayor, Schroeder was determined to protect Oscoda's residents; he finally decided to take action of his own. On Friday, he ordered Ben Chapman, the Iosco County

Sheriff, to arrest any black male found in Oscoda after sunset and keep him in jail overnight. He'd be released the next day.

Colonel Breckenridge was irritated by the mayor's order; less because of its substance than because he hadn't been consulted in advance.

Breckenridge called Wurtsmith's fourteen black officers into his office after he reviewed the mayor's curfew order. He explained the situation, and told them to avoid any confrontation with the civil authorities until the killer was arrested.

"I want you men to pass the word to the other Negroes on base. They should keep their black asses out of town until this thing blows over. Especially at night. Y'all understand?"

The men exchanged glances. Someone cleared his throat. No one said a word. "Anybody got any questions?" Breckenridge asked, raising his voice.

"Not a question, sir," it was Major Cunningham from the legal office. He was the senior black officer present. "Only a comment sir. May I speak freely?"

"Certainly. What is it, Major?"

"This is bullshit, sir. You can't restrict every Negro male to the base just because you've got one Negro suspect. And it's not only bullshit, it's also unconstitutional, sir. In all due respect." Cunningham stared hard at the wing commander. Several others silently nodded their assent.

Breckenridge leaned back in his chair looking at

Cunningham. The room was deathly silent. "You're entitled to your opinion, Major," he said quietly after a
moment. "But that's the way it's going to be. I'm not putting anything in writing, but I want y'all to make sure all
the Negros on base get the word." He took a long drag
on his cigar and deliberately exhaled a cloud of swirling white smoke. The two officers' eyes were locked.
Breckenridge finally broke the silence. "All right, dismissed," he said, nodding toward the door. He kept his
eyes on Cunningham until the major finally turned to
leave. The other officers followed him.

The Bear Track Inn was an old log-cabin roadhouse
on Saginaw Bay, a thirty-minute drive south of Oscoda.
A seven-foot stuffed black bear loomed inside the front
door, greeting guests with a frozen snarl. The bar's inside
walls were covered with eighty years' collection of musty
pelts, antlers, and animal heads. A huge stone fireplace,
always filled with blazing logs in the winter, provided the
heat for the handful of customers, mostly regulars, who'd
venture out on those nights.

In the summertime The Bear Track's patrons were
a mixed group of campers, other vacationers and local
residents. But in the winter, which usually began in early
October, there were only two types of customers, the occasional small groups from the Air Force Base, and the
heartiest local woodsmen, trappers and farmers. Men

who knew that, in deepest winter, the best and sometimes the only way to travel through the countryside was still by dog sled.

A group of officers and their wives were there that Saturday night. Bob Cunningham and his wife, Sandra, had invited Tony and Karen to join them, since everyone new to Wurtsmith, he explained should be properly introduced to The Bear Track. But there was another reason the group went there that night, rather than to one of the bars in Oscoda; to avoid Mayor Schroeder's curfew. Cunningham and the other blacks wouldn't be bothered at The Bear Track.

Sven and Maria Wilcoxon owned and ran The Bear Track. The local legend was that Sven won it from its previous owner in a desperate three-day poker game in 1939. The prior owner, despondent after losing his inn and his life savings, stood up after the last hand, took a shotgun off the wall, and blew his brains out. You could still see the blood stains on the wooden floor where he fell, legend had it. Sven never denied the story, just laughed and walked away whenever he was asked about it.

Sven worked the bar these days, Maria handled the kitchen and a chubby woman named Emma who lived nearby with her parents helped Maria and washed the dishes on busy evenings. Laurie McAllister was their only wintertime waitress, an attractive brunette in her early thirties, who knew all the regulars by name, and was confident enough to flirt with a dozen of them at the same time. Everyone knew that Sheriff Ben Chapman was her boyfriend, but many men came to The Bear Track just to have Laurie add some spark and warmth to a long winter.

"Charlie!" An officer at the far end of their table shouted, "Do you remember that bartender in Izmir? The big guy at the Officers' Club?"

"The one-eyed Turk? Sure. I think I stiffed him the last time I was there. He'd been double-billing us all week-end, so I made it up to him at the very end. Right after I ordered the champagne." Charlie Watson, a crew-cut captain sitting across from Tony, leaned back in his chair and laughed.

"Well, you'd better not go back to Izmir for a while. He's the goddamn mayor now, and he'll probably have you beheaded."

"I'd like to propose a toast" Bob Cunningham announced as he stood up, shouting down the laughter. He raised his glass toward the Jeffries. "To the new prisoners of the Ice Palace, Tony and Karen Jeffries."

"Hear! Hear!"

The group from the base spoke of many things that evening; their travels were a common thread. Tony was amazed to learn how much of the world the others had seen. To Tony, who'd spent most of his life in and near the Chicago area, a trip to the East Coast to visit relatives or to see Washington was an adventure. The men and women with him and Karen that night had lived in places all over the world; with names like Misawa, Heilbronn, and Saigon. And most of the men had spent time in a place called Thule, which, Tony gathered, was a lot further north than Oscoda.

"Let me tell you something about military people, Tony," Bob Cunningham said quietly after Laurie had served them another round of draft beers. "These people, the professionals, move often; never anywhere more than three years, often less. They're the modern American nomads, who rarely put down roots because they've got to always be ready to move on. They make friends quickly, because there isn't time for the usual social minuet found in conventional society. By the end of the evening tonight, you and Karen will be among their best friends." He paused, and added with a smile, "As long as you buy a round or two, that is."

"Advice noted." Tony returned the smile, dug into his pocket, and threw a ten dollar bill into the center of the table. He knew he had six bucks left. "Here" he said loud enough to be heard by everyone. "Our contribution to the kitty."

"Hear! Hear!" Charlie Watson said from across the table, raising his glass to Tony. The others followed.

During a lull in the conversation, Tony turned to Bob Cunningham. "Bob," he asked, "I've heard a lot about the 379th Bomb Wing, the wing's officers, and the wing's mission. But isn't there a base commander too? If there is, I certainly haven't heard anything about him, or how he fits into the scheme of things."

"Sure there's a base commander," Cunningham replied after taking a swig of his beer. "That's Colonel Todd. He has an office down the hall from the wing commander,

Colonel Breckenridge. It's smaller, of course. You have to understand," he added with a smile, "that at a base like Wurtsmith, the wing commander is really in charge. The Base Commander essentially works for him. His responsibility is to ensure that the bomb wing and any other tenant military units have everything they need to operate efficiently. But all the big decisions are made by the wing commander."

"Thanks, Bob. I appreciate the explanation."

Later that evening, Tony learned that Bob Cunningham had been editor-in-chief of the Law Review at Stanford Law School. He'd graduated near the top of his class, but couldn't get a job, or even a serious interview, at any of the major law firms. So he'd decided to make a career as a Judge Advocate in the Air Force, and he'd done well. By now he had probably tried more cases than any of his contemporaries at Stanford had in civilian life. As a major with ten years seniority, he was now almost always involved in serious cases, sometimes assigned as prosecutor and other times as defense counsel. He enjoyed his work.

"It sounds to me like the Air Force treats people pretty fairly," Tony said.

"Well, fairness is a relative term," Cunningham replied quietly, looking away. Tony saw a hardness creep across his face.

They both downed another swig of beer. A couple of chairs away one of the wives was energetically describing a confrontation she'd had with a shopkeeper in Bangkok.

Karen, leaning forward across the table, was laughing at every turn of the story.

Cunningham looked down at his glass, swirling the beer around slowly. "Let's not get into something as serious as fairness," he said quietly. "Let's talk, instead, about something light and frothy." He looked up at Tony, "like murder."

"You mean the Wilton case?"

"Exactly. What do you know about it?"

"I really don't know much about the case at all," Tony said with a shrug. "Except that a rape and murder occurred on base a couple of weeks ago; a girl named Peggy Wilton who worked at the Officers' Club,"

"Let me fill you in a little bit."

This was the first time that Tony had heard the details. It was a grisly crime, its shock waves still reverberating through the community. A pair of supposed eyewitnesses had identified the suspect as a black man, which meant that he had to be connected with the Air Force. Every OSI agent on base was working around the clock trying to identify the murderer, and Cunningham suspected that they'd get their man soon. When they did, there would be a big, high-profile trial held, probably right there at Wurtsmith. If it was, Bob Cunningham knew one way or another he'd be involved.

He explained to Tony that Air Force regulations prohibited prosecutors from outranking defense counsel in Courts Martial. That kept them from intimidating lower ranking defense counsel and gave the prosecution and defense a fairly even footing. Since Cunningham was a major, and the most experienced Air Force trial lawyer around, he assumed that he'd be appointed defense counsel and that someone else from another Base would be brought in to prosecute. The apprehension Tony felt welling up must have shown, because Cunningham told him not to worry. There was no way a rookie lieutenant was going to be appointed to either side of a case of such magnitude.

"What about Lieutenant Colonel Goldsmith?" Tony asked. "Won't he be involved in the trial? Maybe as defense counsel, with you as the prosecutor?"

"No," Cunningham answered with a laugh. "Mel Goldsmith is the Staff Judge Advocate. His job is to make sure that the charges are properly brought, and to act as the Law Officer during the trial. Besides, Mel would be scared to death to try a case like this."

Tony was puzzled by that last comment. He waited while Laurie set down another round of beers, then leaned forward and asked, "What did you mean by that?"

"Tony, Mel Goldsmith may be a lieutenant Colonel with twenty years' experience in the military, but he's only been a lawyer for less than four years. He was a personnel officer most of his career, and took a series of night-school law courses. He finally picked up a law degree at one of his last bases, Selfridge, because it was within driving distance of Wayne State in Detroit. He got admitted to the Nebraska Bar while he was on a brief assignment to Omaha. He figured he'd do better in the Air

Force with a law degree on his resume, and he probably was right. But he's never tried a case, and he's not about to start now."

"Well, what do you know?" Tony sat back, smiling. "You mean he's not any more experienced in trial work than I am?"

"That's right. Don't spread it around, though. Mel's a good guy, and he's sensitive about that. But I thought, as another lawyer, you should know where he's coming from. Don't let him bullshit you."

"Thanks for the advice." Tony raised his glass to Bob Cunningham and took a deep draft. It was deliciously cold. *They probably keep the kegs outside*, he thought.

The fire in the great stone fireplace had burned a little low, so Sven Wilcoxon came out from behind the bar and threw in four new logs, each of which kicked up a swirling storm of glowing sparks as it hit the fire. Within seconds, the fire was blazing again, spreading new warmth across the room.

"Tony, let me tell you something about litigation," Cunningham said. He turned his chair slightly, leaned back and gazed into the fire. He seemed to enjoy the role of mentor. "There are very few things more exciting than taking a tough case, planning it out, then having the pieces fall into place the way you've planned, trying it and winning it. That's exhilarating! It comes in damn close to good sex."

Tony smiled; this man enjoyed his work, and he was probably good at it, too. Tony hoped that Bob Cunningham was right, that he'd be defending the murder case. Tony wanted to watch how a real professional worked in court.

About midnight, Charlie Watson looked at his watch and said that they should take the newcomers back to the base to watch the MITO takeoff. Everyone agreed. They finished their drinks, checked to see that the money on the table would far exceed their bill, and began to bundle up.

"What's a MITO takeoff?" Karen whispered to Tony as she buttoned up her coat.

Bob Cunningham was standing next to them, helping Sandra on with her parka. He turned to Karen and laughed. "It's the most impressive, awe-inspiring thing you've ever seen in your life," he said. "And that's an understatement!"

They said good-bye to Laurie, Emma and the Wilcoxons and piled into their cars for the ride back to the base. Tony and Karen rode with the Cunningham's.

The road north to Oscoda was deserted except for the little convoy of cars from The Bear Track. No other cars were on the road and most of the few snow-covered homes they passed in the moonlight were dark and still. The only signs of life were the occasional deer darting into the underbrush as the convoy approached.

They slowed as they approached the Base, stopping at the gate to be identified. The war protestors were all gone. Tony wondered, *I wonder where people like that go on nights around here, when it might get to be twenty or thirty below? Oh well*, Tony concluded, *that's their problem, not mine*. As they proceeded toward the flight line,

Tony noticed that all the Base's B-52's were either on the runway or on the adjacent taxiway. The roar of their warming engines echoed off the distant line of fir trees.

"What in the hell is going on?" Tony shouted from the back seat of Bob Cunningham's Chevy as they turned down a snow-covered maintenance road on the outside of the fence that paralleled the main runway. Glancing back, he could see the bobbing lights of the other cars swinging in behind them.

"This is an exercise," Cunningham shouted back. "The entire wing's on alert, not just one squadron. This is the way it was during Cuba. Sometime soon, they're going to get the word. When that happens, the whole wing's got to be off the ground within five minutes."

"That's impossible!" Tony protested. "There are thirty-six bombers out there."

"You'll see," Cunningham replied with a smile.

Near the end of the runway their caravan slowed to a stop. Tony and Karen joined the dozen or so others who spilled from the cars. A couple of the men had had the foresight to bring half-pints from The Bear Track, which they passed around to help ward off the intense cold.

Suddenly, Tony heard a distant bell. He looked back at the hangar area, far down the runway. Men were running and lights were flashing. The bombers were lined up in two long rows, one row on the main runway and the other on the parallel taxiway.

The roar of the planes' engines increased, and Tony realized that they were moving forward. *All of them!*

All at once! As the row on the main runway cleared the hangar area, the planes on the taxi-way, already moving forward, pulled in behind them. The entire 379th Bomb Wing, fully loaded and ready for war, was rolling down the runway, steadily picking up speed. They were all taking off simultaneously!

"MITO means Minimum Interval Take-Off," Bob Cunningham shouted in Tony's ear. He could hardly hear him above the crushing noise of the three hundred jet engines coming toward them.

The planes kept building up speed as they roared down the runway. The swirling air currents they created caused an occasional wing tip to almost scrape the runway. But not one plane faltered. If one had, the destructive pileup would have been unimaginable. The bombers lifted off the runway, like thundering dragons, right near the spot where the little group of spectators was watching. As they cleared the trees west of the runway, the huge planes began spreading out. Visible now only by the glow from their navigation lights, some pulled to the right, some to the left, some went straight ahead and climbed rapidly while others roared ahead but hugged the ground.

"They're dispersing," Cunningham yelled. "If we were really at war, the Russians wouldn't fire directly at the Base, but would probably aim a missile for an air burst just above the end of the runway. They'd hope to catch the whole wing together in the air. Now that they're dispersed, the planes won't see each other again until they return."

Tony was speechless. He'd never seen anything like this. Karen turned to look at him, shaking her head in wonderment.

By now the roar of the engines began to fade.

Charlie Watson looked at his watch and smiled. "Four minutes and fifteen seconds from alert to dispersal," he said. "That should make the old man happy."

Bob Cunningham explained to Tony and Karen what the rest of the exercise would entail. The bombers would be refueled over the Arctic Circle, proceed to their Fail-Safe points, and turn back. They wouldn't return to Wurtsmith, because the assumption was that Wurtsmith would be wiped out in a real war's first nuclear exchange. The bombers would head instead to Alpena, some sixty miles to the north. Alpena officials thought the federal government was being generous when it offered to construct a large municipal airport for them twenty years ago, far larger than the small number of general aviation flights into or out of Alpena seemed to justify. But the feds weren't being generous at all. The runway and control tower at Alpena Municipal Airport were exact replicas of Wurtsmith's. At that very moment, Cunningham told Tony and Karen, some two hundred key Wurtsmith personnel were racing toward Alpena in jeeps to escape the anticipated nuclear blast and to activate the recovery facilities. The lead jeep had a machine gun mounted on its hood. In wartime, anyone interfering with that high-speed convoy would be shot, whether in a squad car, a hunter's pickup, or a school bus.

Tony found it interesting that there were no lawyers among those "key" personnel.

Many of the men on base, Cunningham went on, were now either with the wing in the air, or on the way to Alpena to activate the recovery base.

That was a fact that became critical to Mitch Pawlowski's investigation of Peggy Wilton's murder.

—*mm*—

It was after two a.m. when Laurie McAllister finished cleaning up and was able to leave The Bear Track Inn. It had been a good night; she'd made almost eighty dollars in tips. Still, her legs were tired, and she was looking forward to getting home and crawling into bed. Maybe Ben would stop by and help keep her warm. She smiled as she thought about that.

She and Ben had been together for almost four years, and he often stopped by late at night after the Sheriff's office closed.

She drove up the highway toward Oscoda, dropped off Emma before turning left on Johnson Road. The snow plows had been through, and driving was easy, even on the side roads. It was a dark night, the moon was covered by clouds, and there were no lights to be seen anywhere.

Laurie saw a distant flash in her rearview mirror; another car. As it got closer, Laurie saw that the right headlight was slightly dimmer than the left. She knew that car; it was Ben Chapman's County squad car. She leaned back and felt a warm sensation come over her; it would be nice to have Ben in bed with her tonight. She slowed down as she turned into her driveway, easing her car to a stop. Through the trees, she could see that Ben's car was only a couple of hundred yards behind.

Laurie left the door ajar when she walked into the house, turning on the lights. She dropped her coat on the chair in the living room, kicked off her boots, and opened a cabinet to get the bottle of Cutty Sark that she kept for Ben. She heard his car glide to a stop in front; then its door opened and shut. She poured two glasses and began unbuttoning her blouse, her back to the door. She would give him a nice surprise. When she heard the door swing open behind her, she opened her blouse and turned around with a smile.

But it wasn't Ben. And the vehicle parked outside wasn't a squad car.

Chapter 4

———

B en Chapman pulled into Laurie McAllister's driveway a little before ten that Sunday morning. He had
been up all night dealing with a bad accident in Tawas City.
Four men from Detroit, returning from a hunting trip in
the Upper Peninsula, apparently drinking, had broadsided
a car full of teenagers pulling out of the Tastee-Freeze
parking lot. The hospital quickly ran out of blood and Ben
had to drive to Bay City for more. He was exhausted, and
was looking forward to a quiet drink with Laurie, a little
sex and falling asleep in bed with his arms around her.
His Sheriff's hat lay on the front seat beside him.

Ben's legs ached as he climbed the three steps to
Laurie's little front porch. It was a bright day; the sun
glistening off the snow made his tired eyes squint. He
stretched while he tried to decide whether to knock or use
his key and just walk in. He noticed that the wooden door
was ajar, which surprised him, Laurie was usually pretty
careful.

Ben pushed the door and it swung further open.

"Laurie," he called out. "You up?"

He waited a moment in silence before pushing the door the rest of the way open and stepping in.

"Oh my God," he whispered.

The darkened living room was a shambles. Tables and chairs were overturned and broken, shattered glass littered the floor, and gray smears made grotesque patterns on the walls. The curtains were still drawn, but one of them had been torn down, letting a little sunlight into one corner of the room. Ben felt for the light switch next to the door and turned it on. He saw that the smears on the walls were red.

"Laurie?"

Ben instinctively drew his service revolver as he walked slowly across the living room. The house was cold; he had never been there before when it was cold. Pieces of glass crunched beneath his boots. He could smell scotch. And he could also smell something else. It was the faint but distinctive odor that had been with him all night; the smell of blood.

Ben held his .38 in front of him as he pushed open the kitchen door with his left hand. He stepped into the sunlit room, then recoiled in horror.

There on the floor, surrounded by a bright red pool, was Laurie McAllister's mutilated naked body. She was covered with bruises and blood stains, and her throat was cut so deeply that her head had almost been severed. Then Ben saw something else. The brown leather handle of a hunting knife protruded from her vagina.

He turned and staggered toward the bathroom, bile rising in his throat. He dropped his revolver and collapsed in front of the toilet, vomiting into the bowl.

After a few minutes he stood, shaking, trying to pull himself together. He wiped his face off with a towel, and flushed the toilet. Finally, he took a deep breath, picked up his revolver, and walked through the living room and out the front door. He never looked back.

———

The Medical Examiner's report estimated the time of Laurie McAllister's death as being between two and three a.m., January 29th. It described her numerous wounds in stark clinical detail. The knife left in her was one of six hundred similar hunting knives the Base Exchange had sold over the past two years. They hadn't maintained a list of purchasers. Mitch Pawlowski received the report Monday morning; after quickly reviewing, it he took it directly to the Wing Commander.

Alex Breckenridge was seething with anger when Pawlowski walked into his office.

"Damn it, Mitch," he shouted, "Schroeder's on his way right now. If we don't get a handle on this thing today, there's going to be all hell to pay! Do your goddamn job; arrest somebody!"

"We're doing everything we can, Colonel, but we can't make an arrest without some evidence. We've made some progress, but we're still not at the point where we have probable cause to arrest anyone yet."

"What kind of progress?" Breckenridge demanded.

"Well, it's pretty clear that both murders were committed by the same man. They're too similar."

"I agree," Breckenridge snapped. "But where does that get you?"

"Where it gets us, Colonel, is that we've been able to cut our suspect list in the Wilton case down from five to three. Sergeants Nance and Wallace were with the wing in the air Saturday night and Sunday morning, so we know it couldn't have been either of them who killed the McAllister woman. I have my men checking right now on the whereabouts of the other three."

"Well, they sure as hell better come up with something pretty fast," Breckenridge fumed. "Schroeder is about ready to ask the FBI to take over the case. He's calling us goddamned incompetent, and everything else he can think of."

He paced back and forth behind his desk for a few seconds, turned and pointed his finger at Pawlowski. "I'm *not* going to have my career screwed up over this incident, Mitch. This has been *your* responsibility from the beginning. If anyone gets burned over this thing, it's going to be you; not me! Do you understand?"

"Now hold your horses, Colonel," Pawlowski answered, his face flushed with anger. "We've been bustin' our goddamn butts on this investigation..."

He was interrupted by a loud knock on the door.

Breckenridge's aide stuck his head in, "Special Agent Dan Kula from the OSI is outside, Colonel. He'd like to see both of you."

"Send him in," Breckenridge shouted. He shot a glare at Pawlowski, then sat down behind his desk.

A moment later, Dan Kula strode into the room and gave the wing commander a brisk salute. Unlike his boss, Pawlowski, Kula always wore his uniform, unless he was off base on special assignment.

"At ease, sergeant," Breckenridge said, returning his salute. "What do you have for us?"

"It's about the murders, sir." Turning to Pawlowski, he continued. "We checked on the other three suspects from the first murder, as you ordered. Two of them, Sergeant Bowan and Airman Dawson were with the secondary recovery team in Alpena Saturday night; they left the base about ten minutes after the initial recovery team left, which you led Colonel, after picking up any key personnel who had missed the first recovery convoy; after that only one of the three was on base; Airman Second Class Torrance. George Torrance."

"He's our goddamn man! Has to be!" Breckenridge said, slamming both hands down on his desk. "Pick him up right now!"

"Now wait a minute, Colonel," Pawlowski said. "This is a nice break. But let's think this through and be sure we're right. We don't want to screw things up and move on the wrong man." He paused a moment, "Let's go through the timing. The primary recovery convoy left here about twelve-thirty Saturday night, didn't it?"

"Twelve thirty-five," Breckenridge snapped. "I was in the lead jeep."

"Do you recall what time you got to Alpena?"

"One-fifteen. We were barreling. But what the hell's the point of this, Mitch?" The Colonel's voice rose as he spoke.

Turning to Kula, Pawlowski asked, "Dan, how long does it usually take to drive from here to Alpena or back? Without the sirens."

"About an hour this time of year, if the roads are open. Like they were Saturday night."

"We've got a problem, Colonel," Pawlowski said. "The Medical Examiner put the McAllister woman's time of death at between two and three a.m. Either of those other two men, Brown or Dawson, could have gone to Alpena with the secondary recovery convoy, checked in, and come back here in one of the jeeps with plenty of time to kill her. We don't have any real evidence that it was Torrance."

"Bullshit!" Breckenridge shouted as he quickly rose to his feet. "Torrance has been a bum from day one. I know that man. He's been court martialed before. He's always getting the colored airmen riled up over something or another. We should have thrown him out long before this! No, there's no doubt about it, he's exactly the type who would do something like this. And now we have the proof, enough proof for me!"

"Colonel, let me question him before we do anything,"

Pawlowski protested. "He might have an iron-clad alibi for Saturday night."

Before Breckenridge could answer, Mayor Carl Schroeder stormed into the room, pulling off his gloves. "Another woman raped and murdered," he shouted. "I've had enough of this! Have you identified the killer or not?" He glared at Breckenridge across his desk. "Because if you haven't, I'm going to insist that the FBI step in, and take this investigation over. Today!"

"Yes, Carl, we have," Breckenridge answered calmly, sitting down. "I was just about to call you."

Schroeder straightened up, blinked and stepped back slightly.

"Mr. Pawlowski here has just concluded that it had to be Airman Second Class George Torrance. Fine bit of police work, if I must say so. Torrance is the only man on base who fits the description of the killer, and who could have been at the scene of both crimes. Isn't that right, Mitch?"

Mitch Pawlowski took a deep breath, looked hard at Breckenridge then turned to the Mayor. "Yes," he said. "Airman Torrance is the one. Can't be anyone else. Special Agent Kula and I are on our way to arrest him right now."

※※※

The Wurtsmith Air Force Base Officers' Club was the largest building on base besides the aircraft hangars.

Outside, the concrete-block walls were a drab gray; but inside, the decor equaled that of the finest country clubs. When Curtis LeMay built the northern tier of SAC Bases, he made sure that his men would have the finest amenities while serving in those remote locations.

Deep pile carpeting, pine-paneled walls, subdued lighting and polished brass fixtures set the Club's tone. The dining room served the best food and had the best wine list found anywhere within one hundred miles. Fresh seafood and live lobsters were flown in twice a week on training flights to the Azores. The bar, with padded leather chairs, was reasonable as well as comfortable. A man could lay down a ten-dollar bill, drink good bourbon or scotch all evening, leave a decent tip, and still walk out with change.

As in many country clubs, Wurtsmith's front hall was lined with framed photographs of distinguished gentlemen associated with the premises. Unlike civilian clubs, however, Wurtsmith's photos weren't of past club presidents, but were of all the men in the Base's chain-of-command, beginning with the wing commander, Colonel Alex Breckenridge, and running up through the Commander-in-Chief, President Lyndon Johnson.

The wing commander and his executive officer, Major James Lee Davis, arrived at the Officers' Club about six that Monday evening. It had been a hectic day, but a satisfying one. The 379th Bomb Wing had returned from its exercise over the Arctic Circle, landing first in Alpena, before making the short hop down to Wurtsmith.

The Club's bar was filled with the exuberant flight crews. Everyone felt it had gone well, and were confident the wing would receive a good rating. But more importantly to Breckenridge was that the murderer had been identified and arrested. He had to be punished, swiftly and sternly. No stupid local scandal was going to screw up his career.

He and Davis agreed that it was essential that Airman Torrance be convicted. He'd promised that to Mayor Schroeder, and he didn't want any bad surprises now that the crimes had been solved.

They found Mel Goldsmith at his usual place at the bar and took him aside for some private conversation over drinks. Mel was old school; they knew they could rely on him.

"Mel," Jimmy Davis asked as they sat down at a corner table "who's the best prosecutor in SAC? The very best. If you had to win one case, who would you want to prosecute it?" Alex Breckenridge sat back to listen, swirling his Jack Daniels on the rocks.

Mel Goldsmith thought for a moment. He knew why they were asking. "Donovan," he said finally. "Tom Donovan. He's stationed at Omaha right now. He's a senior captain, and will probably make major this spring. I don't think he's ever lost a case."

"Could you, or could we, arrange to get him temporarily assigned here to prosecute the Torrance case?" Davis asked.

"Probably. As long as you're willing to work around his schedule. He's in demand."

"That shouldn't be any problem at all, should it, Colonel?" Davis looked at the wing commander, who quietly shook his head.

"All right, I'll put in a call tomorrow," Goldsmith answered as he finished off his vodka martini and gestured to a waiter for another. "He'll get the job done for you. I'll guarantee that."

"Now, what about the defense counsel?" Davis continued. "Who is that likely to be?"

"Torrance can hire his own counsel, if he's got the money," Goldsmith replied. What kind of dough does he have?"

"Zero, from what I can gather," Davis answered. "He owes money all over the Base. Whoever we appoint is going to be his lawyer. It's got to be Bob Cunningham. He's the only lawyer around with the experience and rank to try a case like this against Tom Donovan. Remember, since Donovan's a captain, the defense attorney has to be at least a captain."

"I don't want it to be Cunningham," Breckenridge said, leaning forward. "The guy's got an attitude problem. He'd try to figure out some way of stickin' it to us."

"Mel, let me put it another way," Davis said, glancing quickly around the room. "Bob Cunningham's too good." He was speaking very softly. "Look, we know this guy's guilty. We don't want any chance of the defense counsel pulling some damn lawyer's trick and getting Torrance off." He was almost whispering now.

"Jimmy," Mel Goldsmith answered, just as quietly.

"If Cunningham is here, we'll have to appoint him. We'll draw all kinds of fire if we don't, and that won't be good for any of us." His raised eyebrow made the point better than his words. "We'll have to find some way to get Cunningham transferred out of here, at least temporarily. That can be arranged, can't it, Colonel?"

Breckenridge silently nodded.

One of the officers from the flight crews stopped by to exchange a few words. He joked about how they'd had trouble locating their refueling tanker over Greenland on the return flight that afternoon. He downed the last of his drink and went back to the bar for a refill.

"Now, Mel," Davis continued quietly after the pilot left "who's the most inexperienced rookie lawyer you could get your hands on, to appoint as defense counsel for Airman Torrance?"

"Well, the new guy, of course. Jeffries. But he's only a first lieutenant, not a captain."

"Then we'll make Tony Jeffries a captain," Davis replied with a devilish grin. "Call it a battlefield promotion. That's within your discretion, isn't it, Colonel?"

"A promotion to captain? It sure as hell is." Colonel Breckenridge smiled as he unwrapped a long dark Panamil. Major Davis leaned forward to light the wing commander's cigar. "Thank you, Jimmy," Breckenridge said. He leaned back and exhaled a cloud of white smoke. "All right, that's the plan. Our Lieutenant Jeffries will be promoted to captain and will defend the murder case. Yes, I like it."

As Breckenridge began to rise, Goldsmith raised his hand slightly. "Colonel," he said, "do you think we should get Colonel Todd involved in this? He *is* the Base Commander.

"Todd? That candy-ass? No!" Breckenridge responded forcefully as he sat back down. "First of all, I'm the ranking officer on base, and that wimp wouldn't dare try to countermand an order of mine. And second, he'd probably screw it up somehow and the blame would end up on my shoulders. No, Todd's involved only on a need-to-know basis. Now, gentlemen, if you'll excuse me," he said as he rose, "I'd like to talk to some of the men who made us look good today."

When Tony arrived at the legal office the next morning, Tuesday, he was surprised to find the waiting room filled with men. The 922nd Helicopter Rescue Squadron, also stationed at Wurtsmith for rescue operations in northern Lake Huron, had received orders that they were being sent to Viet Nam that afternoon. They needed choppers in Nam and the 922nd was picked to go. Everyone in the squadron was advised that he should report to the legal office to write a new Will before he left. Those who were married were also told to fill out and sign a Power of Attorney for their wives. The 922nd would be in Da Nang in thirty-six hours.

Tony knew a few of the men. He hadn't realized that

Charlie Watson was a helicopter pilot. Mike Jablonski, who lived with his wife, Sally, in the apartment next to Tony and Karen, was also there. Sally was expecting their first baby in the spring, and they were hoping to have their house by April.

Mel Goldsmith and Bob Cunningham had dealt with this type of situation before. Goldsmith had Ruth Olmsted pass out forms to everyone, asking them to list the basic information the attorneys would need in preparing the documents. Tony was given simple Will and Power of Attorney forms that he should follow. There was no fancy estate planning involved and no time to formulate elaborate trusts or special bequests. The Wills would be individually typed, signed and witnessed, but they would all have a certain similarity: "Everything to my wife, _____ if she survives me; if not, then to my surviving children in equal shares." Some had a little more, but not much. The Powers of Attorney were just as terse.

While they were waiting, a number of the sergeants were reading manuals they received that morning. They were the crew chiefs of the helicopters. The manuals instructed them how to install .50-caliber machine guns in their birds while they were being flown to Viet Nam in the bellies of C-124 cargo planes. When they arrived in Da Nang the blades in their choppers would be reattached, ammunition for the guns distributed, and they would be immediately thrown into action supporting the First Marine Division. Their role, however, would not be air-sea rescue as it had been in Michigan, but combat support.

There was a problem though, that no one in the Pentagon had thought through. Helicopters designed for combat support are built with as much armor as possible around the pilots and gunners. Air-sea rescue helicopters, on the other hand, have the crew surrounded by windows to maximize their fields of vision. Whoever in the Pentagon made the decision to send the 922nd into combat apparently was unaware of that distinction. The helicopters of the 922nd Rescue Squadron had large Plexiglas windows surrounding the crew and no armor.

Of the twenty-seven Last Wills that Tony Jeffries wrote and witnessed that day, twenty-four would "mature" within one month, including the Wills of Captain Charles Watson and First Lieutenant Michael Jablonski. All twenty-four men would be heading home in body bags.

Chapter 5

—*www*—

"What the hell is this?"

Bob Cunningham reread the orders he had just received. He was being temporarily assigned to head up a sonic-boom claims office in Milwaukee. It was a three-month assignment. The orders were signed by Colonel F. X. Reynolds, Staff Judge Advocate of SAC's Second Air Force, headquartered in Barksdale, Louisiana. Bob Cunningham had met Colonel Reynolds a few times, but didn't know him well.

He looked up Colonel Reynold's number in the SAC directory and called him immediately. He was put on hold for several minutes, but finally got through.

"Colonel Reynolds," he said, "This is Major Bob Cunningham at Wurtsmith."

"Good morning, major. How are you?" The reply was friendly enough.

"Fine, Colonel, except for one thing. I've just received orders sending me TDY to Milwaukee for three months. I'd like to talk to you about that."

"Yes," Reynolds answered. "I signed those orders yesterday. This is an important assignment, major, and I'm pleased that you'll be able to handle it. Let me give you the background on this project..."

"Before you do, Colonel," Cunningham cut in, "let me tell you something you probably don't know. We have a murder trial scheduled here in less than a month. The charges were just issued the other day. I'm our only experienced trial lawyer, and this office is going to need me to try one side or the other. We're going to have to scramble to find someone to handle the other side; but for me to leave right now would be very awkward for this office."

"That's the Torrance trial, isn't it? I'm familiar with that case, major, but I'm afraid that it can't override our need to have you in Milwaukee. It'll be a sensitive position there, and we want a man with some maturity to be in charge. Don't worry about the staffing for the Torrance trial; we'll deal with that."

Cunningham was surprised that Colonel Reynolds knew about the Torrance case already. He tried to figure that out while Reynolds prattled on about how the Air Force was working with the Department of Transportation on the Milwaukee project. The temporary office there, Reynolds explained, would be ostensibly processing claims for sonic-boom damage caused by our planes doing practice runs over simulated Russian cities, but its actual role would be to measure the local response to a series of increasingly intense sonic booms over Milwaukee during the next three months. Similar sonic-boom runs would be conducted over half a dozen other major cities during the same period. When the tests were completed the Department of Transportation would have much better data for evaluating the public's resistance to repeated sonic booms and decide whether or not to proceed with the development of an American Super Sonic Transport, similar to the Concord which the British and French were developing. "We'll need a senior man there," Reynolds continued, "who can deal with the questions and objections that are certain to arise without revealing our actual mission."

Bob Cunningham finally seized a chance to speak, "I appreciate the seriousness of that project and the need for a fairly senior officer to respond to the anticipated complaints. But, I'd very much like to be able to handle this murder case here. I'd appreciate it if you'd do me a personal favor and cancel..."

"Out of the question, Cunningham. The orders have been cut already. Besides, you come highly recommended."

"Recommended? Who recommended me for that job, Colonel?" He stood up as he asked the question. He was becoming increasingly uncomfortable with the conversation.

"Can't recall. But that doesn't really matter. Anyway, I'm sure you'll do a fine job. Thanks for the call."

A dial tone was suddenly buzzing in Cunningham's ear. He looked at the receiver, then slowly hung it up. After a moment, he grabbed the orders and strode down the hall to Mel Goldsmith's office.

Goldsmith seemed just as surprised as he was by the transfer orders. He observed, though, that most men would prefer to spend the winter in Milwaukee than in Oscoda.

"I don't mind going to Milwaukee, Mel. But who's going to handle the murder trial? That's a big case, and I was looking forward to being involved. You're going to need two experienced trial lawyers and if I'm gone you're not going to have anybody. If it's handled badly, you could end up with egg all over your face."

"You're absolutely right, Bob," Goldsmith agreed. "I can't spare you right now at all. Look, I'll call Omaha and try to get those orders rescinded. I'll go over Frank Reynolds' head."

But Mel Goldsmith wasn't able to get the temporary assignment orders canceled. At the end of the day he told Cunningham that he had tried every connection and pulled every string he had at SAC Headquarters, but nothing worked. "I'm sorry Bob," Goldsmith continued, "this completely blind-sided me, too. I'm going to have a hell of a hard time filling those two slots for the murder trial, but I'll figure it out somehow. The fact is, though, that you're going to have to go to Milwaukee immediately. One consolation, if it helps, is that Sandra and your two youngsters will be able to accompany you."

Before Bob could respond, Goldsmith's phone rang; he took it and waved Bob off. Their conversation was over. Bob paused, turned and left, trying to figure out what the hell was going on.

—◊◊◊—

The 40th Air Division had General Court Martial Convening Authority covering Wurtsmith and its Order authorizing the General Court Martial of George Torrance came through the first week of February. It gave broad discretionary power to Colonel Breckenridge to appoint the members of the Court Martial Panel, and appointed Captain Thomas Donovan as the prosecutor.

—◊◊◊—

Tom Donovan was sitting in his office in SAC Headquarters at Offutt Air Force Base outside Omaha, when he learned he was being sent to Wurtsmith to prosecute a murder case scheduled to begin trial on February twenty-first. Normally, he'd have objected to being sent to one of the northern-tier bases at that time of year. But this was a murder case. Murder cases are always something special for a prosecutor. Donovan had never ducked a case; nor had he ever lost one. He checked his calendar and saw that he was free that week and the following week.

Tom Donovan was a native of Winnetka, Illinois, and the son of a wealthy Chicago commodities broker. As a youngster, he'd enjoyed a comfortable life; he'd been to Europe three times before graduating from New Trier High School. He attended Princeton and Yale Law

School before joining Air Force JAG to get his military commitment out of the way. When his initial term was up, he decided to stay on, to his parents' surprise. But Tom Donovan had no need to chase wealth, nor the desire to engage in the frenzied competition of the large law firms. There was a certain excitement in being in the military. Besides, he loved trying cases, which he was doing on a regular basis, while his Yale classmates were still either wrestling with arcane issues in dusty law libraries or sitting in second chairs at mundane trials that ultimately resulted in a financial exchange between two large banks or insurance companies.

After eight years in the Air Force and almost a hundred Courts Martial, Tom Donovan had become a very good trial lawyer indeed. In fact, he was the only Air Force JAG officer who had been admitted as a Fellow in the American College of Trial Lawyers. An attractive man of six feet and 175 pounds, he had a commanding presence in a courtroom.

As his experience and reputation grew, Donovan had been increasingly called on to prosecute tough cases on other bases. A year ago, in 1967, he was named Chief Prosecutor of SAC's Second Force and was rumored to be on the next list of appointments to Major.

Tom Donovan began looking forward to prosecuting the murder case against Airman George Torrance at Wurtsmith Air Force Base. It would give him the opportunity to add another trophy to his collection.

Tony was swamped with work within days after Major Cunningham left for Milwaukee. He had never realized how many reports, opinion letters and recommendations were expected from the Wing Legal Office. Nor had he appreciated the volume of work that Bob Cunningham handled. Most of that was now his responsibility. He had grown to admire and respect Cunningham in the short time they had worked together; but now he'd developed a new level of respect, a better sense of how good a lawyer Bob Cunningham really was. Tony found that he was taking days to write reports that Cunningham was clearly able to get out in a couple of hours.

One morning, shortly after he arrived at work, Tony got a call to report to the Wing Commander's office. Ruth Olmsted phoned it to him while he was still savoring his first cup of coffee, and he could tell from the tone of her voice that this was something unusual. He'd met Colonel Breckenridge only once when Mel Goldsmith gave him a full tour of the headquarters building and introduced him to the Base's senior officers the day after he reported. Breckenridge was about the age of Tony's dad, as he recalled, but didn't appear nearly as friendly.

Tony tried to imagine what this meeting could be about as he walked down the long corridor from the Legal Office to the wing commander's wing of the headquarters building. A gnawing anxiety was growing in the pit of his stomach. He hoped he hadn't somehow screwed things up.

When Tony was ushered in, Colonel Breckenridge was seated behind his oversized desk, with the busy activity on the flight line visible through the windows behind him. Mel Goldsmith sat in a smaller arm chair off to one side. They both smiled as they greeted him, Colonel Breckenridge returned his salute and asked Tony to take a seat, gesturing to the empty chair facing his desk. He said that they had some good news for him.

"Jeffries, we've been very impressed with you in the short time that you've been here," Breckenridge began. "Colonel Goldsmith here tells me that you're probably the brightest and best young lawyer he's ever had the opportunity to work with."

Tony was very pleased to hear that; apparently he wasn't in trouble after all. He eased back in his seat and relaxed slightly. He hadn't been sure what sort of an impression he'd been making. He'd been at Wurtsmith only a few weeks, and hadn't yet had a chance to do anything of much consequence.

"You're the kind of young man we want to encourage to stay in the Air Force, son," Breckenridge continued. "I know that this might be a bit early to raise the subject, but when your tour of duty's over we'd like you to seriously consider making a career of the Air Force."

Wow! Tony thought. This was heady stuff. He hadn't planned to stay in the military, but this was very flattering, coming from the wing commander himself. Maybe it was something he should consider.

"And to help you make that decision, son, we're going to put you on the fast track. We want you to rise like an eagle," Breckenridge said, smiling. Tony glanced at Lieutenant Colonel Goldsmith. He too was nodding and smiling.

"I have it within my discretion to make certain promotions," Breckenridge continued. "And I'm exercising that authority right now lieutenant. Jeffries, you're now being promoted to Captain Jeffries, effective immediately!"

Tony was stunned. He didn't know that this sort of thing could happen in the Air Force. But he really didn't know that much about the military. "Thank….., thank you, Colonel," he stammered. "This is very exciting, and…" He paused, groping for words, "…and unexpected."

Mel Goldsmith rose, extending his hand. Tony scrambled to his feet and took it. "Congratulations, *Captain* Jeffries," Goldsmith said smiling and handed Tony a small white box he had been holding. "Here are your captain's insignia. Tracks, we call them." As Tony took the box, Goldsmith continued, "These used to be mine. I've been waiting to pass them on to a real lawyer. You're that man, Tony. Wear them with pride."

Tony was floating. He suddenly realized he was grinning and tried to appear more serious. "I'll do my best to live up to your expectations, sir," he said to Goldsmith. "And yours too, sir," he added to Breckenridge.

"I'm sure you will, son." There was an odd smile on the wing commander's face as he spoke.

"Oh, and while you're here, Tony, we have some more good news for you," Goldsmith said. He pulled a folded piece of paper from inside his coat pocket and handed it to the new captain. "You're being appointed defense counsel in the Court Martial of Airman George Torrance."

"What? The murder case?"

"That's right," Goldsmith replied as he eased back into his chair. "I've talked it over with the Colonel here and he's in full agreement. It's a lot of responsibility, but we wouldn't give it to you if we weren't confident that you can handle it. We know you can." He smiled. "This case will set you down that fast track with a full head of steam."

"Sir, I'm not so sure..." Tony stammered.

"Well, we are, and here's the file on the case." Goldsmith picked a thin folder off the corner of Breckenridge's desk and handed it to Tony. "When you go through it," he added, "you'll notice that the case is set for trial on February twenty-first.

"Sir, I've never tried a case before!" Tony protested.

"Don't worry. You've gone to one of the best law schools in the country," Goldsmith answered. "And as the Colonel said, you're probably the brightest young lawyer I've ever had the pleasure to work with. Captain Jeffries, you'll do just fine." There was a hint of hardness in his voice as he finished.

"Sir," Tony responded, "that's a little less than three weeks from now. Won't I need more time to prepare and to depose the prosecution's witnesses, to examine their proposed exhibits...?"

"No, this isn't civil litigation, Captain Jeffries," Goldsmith said "There's no discovery, no depositions, no review of the other side's proposed exhibits. You get the case. You try it. That's it." Tony's mind was reeling; he didn't have any idea how he was going to proceed or what to say.

Breckenridge leaned back in his chair and puffed on his cigar. He was watching Tony closely.

"And I'll tell you what I'll do," Goldsmith went on. "We have another young lawyer reporting tomorrow, a Lieutenant McDonald. I'll appoint him assistant defense counsel, so you'll have someone to work with. Feel better?"

"A little, yes sir, thank you."

Tony stood there for a moment, uncertain what to do or say. Pieces of questions were tumbling through his mind, none of which could he grasp and articulate.

"Well, son, maybe you'd better start working on your case," Colonel Breckenridge said quietly.

"Right. Yes, sir," Tony said, realizing he had been dismissed. He saluted awkwardly, turned and walked from the room. His head was spinning. A murder trial? *Am I ready to defend a murder trial?*

Tony was in a daze as he walked back down the long hallway to the Legal Office. *What just happened back there? A promotion to captain even though they've never really seen what I can do? And this murder trial assignment? Is this really the way the Air Force works, or is something else going on here?* He just nodded to Ruth Olmsted in response to her friendly greeting as he walked through their reception room. He went into his office, shut the door, and sat down at his desk. The manila folder labeled *"United States vs. George Torrance"* lay in front of him for a long time. Finally, Tony opened it and looked at the formal charges.

"O.K., Tony," he said aloud. "You're a lawyer. Let's see what this case is all about. "

—*mm*—

Mitch Pawlowski was uncomfortable. They had arrested Airman George Torrance based entirely on circumstantial evidence. They had nothing yet to actually link him with either crime. His fingerprints weren't found anywhere in Laurie McAllister's house. In fact, the only fingerprints found were Laurie's and Ben Chapman's. From the smudges, it appeared that the killer had worn thin leather gloves that night.

Pawlowski didn't receive any greater degree of comfort when he inquired into the whereabouts of Staff Sergeant Bowan and Airman Dawson the full night of Laurie McAllister's murder. Both had arrived in Alpena with the recovery team at about one twenty-five a.m., but had no other duties until the following afternoon when the bombers began returning. Either of them could have taken one of the jeeps back to Oscoda in time to murder and rape her and return to Alpena without ever being missed.

Laurie's little house had already been inspected once

by one of Ben Chapman's deputies. But Pawlowski wanted to inspect it again himself; sometimes little things are missed. If he looked closely enough maybe he'd be able to find something to confirm that George Torrance was the killer, or to point to somebody else. Either alternative was acceptable to him. The present state of affairs was not.

He had arranged to meet Sheriff Chapman, who had the key, at Laurie's house at two that afternoon. He drove south on highway 23 through the little village of Au Sable and turned west onto Johnson Road.

Au Sable was even smaller than Oscoda, and virtually closed down in the winter. The temperature was hovering around zero; the high for the day, and with the stiff northeastern wind off Lake Huron, the chill factor was about fifty below.

Chapman was waiting in his car, engine running, when Pawlowski arrived at Laurie's house. The Sheriff unlocked and opened the wooden door for Pawlowski, then turned and said, "Mitch, if you don't mind, and don't need me, I'd rather not go back in there myself."

"I understand," Pawlowski responded. He'd been through enough murder investigations in his life to know how they can affect people close to the victims, even a city cop or a country sheriff. "I'll lock up when I'm done and drop the key off at your office. Thanks for your help."

Chapman nodded in appreciation, returned to his squad car, turned around, and drove off down Johnson Road.

After entering the house Pawlowski took off his jacket, thankful that the furnace was running, and replaced his heavy leather gloves with light cotton ones. He examined Laurie's calendar, correspondence, utility bills and check book taking notes as he proceeded. He carefully moved each piece of furniture to look beneath and behind it, taking dozens of photos, replacing each item exactly as he found it. He dusted for fingerprints in areas that might not have been checked before, like the front porch railing and the water taps in the kitchen and bathroom.

By the time he left at nearly five, he'd found what he was looking for.

Chapter 6

Tony was poring over the Court of Military Appeals' latest opinion affirming a murder conviction when Mel Goldsmith knocked once and pushed open his office door. "Tony, let me introduce you to our new man, Lieutenant Wally McDonald," he said, ushering in a tall young man. "Lieutenant, this is Captain Tony Jeffries."

"Good to meet you, Wally," Tony said as he rose and extended his hand. At a little over six feet, he was a couple inches taller than Tony.

"My pleasure, captain," McDonald responded with a smile. "Colonel Goldsmith said that we're going to be working on a case together."

"That's right," Tony answered. "A serious one. But first, you're going to have to cut out that 'captain' nonsense. It's Tony. I haven't been here much longer than you have. Where are you from?"

"St. Louis. The suburbs, actually - University City."

"Look, I'm going to let you guys get acquainted," Mel

Goldsmith interrupted. "Tony, why don't you show Wally around the shop? His office is going to be the empty one across the hall."

"I'll be happy to," Tony replied.

"Glad to have you here, Lieutenant," Goldsmith said, shaking McDonald's hand on his way out the door.

Tony began the tour by showing McDonald his eight-by-ten cubicle across the corridor. He could tell that McDonald was just as excited as Tony had been when he got his first office. The offices were nearly identical, except that McDonald's faced the drab wooden wall of another wing of their building fifteen feet away while Tony's opened on to the picturesque view of a twelve thousand foot concrete runway. McDonald left his brief-case on the bare metal desk in his office and followed Tony down the hall.

McDonald had a full head of untamed brown hair that he was constantly brushing back from his face. He had graduated from Notre Dame Law School last June, had been admitted to the bar in Missouri and had just completed a six-week orientation course at Lackland Air Force Base in San Antonio. He was married to a wonderful girl named Patty who'd be driving up in two days in her parents' car. As he spoke, Tony wished that he'd been given an orientation course as well, before being sent to an operational base.

They were the same age and they'd both just graduated from law school, but Tony was a captain now and McDonald just a first lieutenant. That made Tony uncomfortable; he felt that he was impersonating a more experienced officer, and that he really should be wearing lieutenants' bars. "It's a fluke, you know, our difference in rank" he observed more than once as he showed McDonald around. "I really don't have any more experience than you."

"Tell me about this case that we'll be working on together," McDonald asked casually as Tony led him through the library.

Tony stopped, stared ahead for a moment, turned and said. "It's a *murder* case. You and I are going to be defending a man charged with double rape and murder in less than three weeks."

"Murder! Hey, that's exciting." A little smile crept across McDonald's face. "How many murder cases have you tried before?"

"Hey, haven't you been listening?" Tony said quietly. "I've never tried a murder case before. I've never defended a petty theft case. I've never even defended a traffic ticket. I just got out of law school, too."

McDonald stared at Tony. He opened his mouth as though he were going to speak, took a deep breath, then shut it. He half-turned, looked away, and shook his head. Finally, he turned back to Tony and whispered, "What's the penalty for murder in the Air Force?"

"Death by firing squad," Tony answered, almost as quietly. "Or twenty years to life, if the court chooses to be lenient."

"Jesus Christ!"

"My sentiments precisely. Now, how much criminal law did you take at Notre Dame?"

"Only the introductory course. My concentration was in taxes."

"Beautiful ."

Tony noticed beads of perspiration appearing on McDonald's forehead and upper lip. It was clear that Wally McDonald wasn't going to be much help at all. Still, he was the only one Tony had to work with.

"Look, I was just about to go over to the stockade to meet the defendant" Tony said as they left the library. "George Torrance is his name. His personnel file is on my desk, Tony gestured toward his office as they approached it. Want to thumb through it and come along?"

"Sure, I'll take some notes." McDonald grabbed the folder and a yellow pad from Tony's desktop and brushed his hair back from his eyes. "Let's go."

"I think we'd better take our coats too," Tony said dryly. "It's about ten below outside."

"Right."

—*ww*—

They took McDonald's car which was parked right in front of the headquarters building. The engine took some coaxing before it finally turned. Tony had walked to work that morning, as he did every day, since their apartment was only a hundred yards away, and he found that you could get very cold walking even that short distance in sub-zero temperatures.

As they drove over to the Air Police Compound, Tony told McDonald that the prosecutor was someone named Tom Donovan. He was being sent in from another base and would arrive about a week before the scheduled start of the trial. Nobody seemed to know much of anything about him; Mel Goldsmith said he'd never heard of the guy.

A powdery white snow was falling, creating black ice and making the roads just slippery enough to be danger-ous. McDonald seemed to be a good driver, keeping their speed low, and slowly easing through the turns. Several times Tony heard him mutter the word "murder" and just shake his head.

They parked and signed in at the stockade, showed their ID's to the sergeant at the front desk and were taken through a doorway to a small conference room down a side corridor. It was about eight feet square, had white concrete-block walls, and contained only a metal table surrounded by four steel folding chairs. A metal ashtray sat near one corner of the table. Through the one narrow barred window Tony could see that light snow was con-tinuing to fall.

After a few minutes a burly NCO brought a tall, thin black man into the room, opened the manacles that chained his wrists together, but kept his foot manacles locked. He directed him to sit, pushing him down into the chair across from Tony for emphasis.

"These are your lawyers, Torrance. You're supposed

to cooperate with 'em." Looking at Tony he added, "When you're done, captain, or if you have any problem, just bang on the door. I'll be right down the hall."

Torrance was about six foot-two, lean and wiry, with a short afro. He had a dusty gray complexion, a nasty scar down the right side of his face, and a black pencil-line mustache. He was dressed in the stockade's standard light green jump suit, with the top three snaps open and his dog tags dangling on his chest. He leaned back in his chair and stared at the two white officers sitting across from him while he massaged his wrists.

"I'm Captain Jeffries, Airman Torrance. This is Lieutenant McDonald. We've been appointed as your defense counsel."

"Both of you?"

"That's right."

Torrance grunted his approval. He seemed pleased to have two lawyers working on his case.

"First of all," Tony said, "I want you to understand that anything you say to us, or that we say to you, is absolutely confidential. It's covered by the attorney-client privilege." Torrance nodded his understanding, and it occurred to Tony that this was probably not the first time that he had heard those words.

"You're being charged with the rape and murder of a young woman named Peggy Wilton on base the night of January 8th, and with the rape and murder of another woman named Laurie McAllister in Au Sable in the early morning of January 29th." Anything you care to tell us about your whereabouts on either or both of those nights?" Tony sat back, watching his new client carefully.

"What a bunch of bullshit!" Torrance responded indignantly, shaking his head. He stared at the ceiling for a moment, leaned forward with both arms on the table and said "Cap'n, let me tell you somethin'. That first night I was with my woman the whole fuckin' time. She drove up here to the base and spent the night. That other night I was at Blake's 'til it closed 'bout four. I got a dozen witnesses. Shit, they ain't got no case against me a'tall." He pulled a pack of Luckies out of his prisoner jumpsuit pocket and lit one up.

"What's Blake's?" Tony asked.

"It's a colored bar," Torrance answered, gesturing over his shoulder. "South of the base down River Road. The sheriff don't hassle colored folk long as we go to Blake's. You go to any other bar roun' here and that sheriff'll hassle the livin' shit out outta you."

"Are you sure you were at Blake's in the early morning of January 29th? The time of the second murder?" Tony asked. McDonald picked up his pad and began taking notes.

"I'm at Blake's every night, cap'n. The only times I ain't been to Blake's the last month or so was when my woman come up and spent the night. Once was that January 8th. I 'member that cause it was a special night. Before that was in December a couple a times."

Tony was encouraged. It sounded like Torrance

might have good alibis for both nights, if they could be confirmed.

"How late is Blake's normally open?" he asked.

Torrance shrugged his shoulders. "Pends on business. Sometimes three. Sometimes four. Sometimes five. Like I say, 'pends."

"And you close the bar every night?"

"Sure, me and a couple other guys. Course, you gotta understan', cap'n," he added with a smile. "I work second shift. So I don't hafta report till 4. In the afternoon, y'understan'? And I be done 'bout midnight. Earlier, if I can swing it, that's when I go to Blake's. Every damn night." Torrance paused. "Let me ask you somethin', cap'n. Both those women were raped, right?"

"That's right," Tony answered.

"So cap'n, why I wanna go and do that? My woman, Lucy, takes care of me every way you can 'magin'. Hell, she the best thing ever happened to me. A real fox! Why would I wanna go out and jump some strange broads and risk gettin' into a shitload of trouble? 'Specially white broads, which I hear they was. I don't need that, cap'n. In fact, it makes no sense at all."

"That's not a bad point," Tony said, leaning back in his chair.

"Wait a minute," McDonald interrupted. He had been thumbing through Torrance's personnel file. "It says here, George, that your wife's name is Ruby and that she lives in Atlanta. This woman, Lucy, she's not your wife, I take it?"

"No, you right," Torrance said, with a shrug. "But what the shit." He slowly ground out his cigarette in the ashtray, looking at McDonald. "Ruby and I was married 'bout six years ago. It was a mistake; we was just a couple of dumb kids. She left me when I was sent overseas. Hell, I don't even know where she is no more. She hasn't lived at that address in years," he said, gesturing toward the personnel folder in McDonald's hands.

"Why didn't you ever get a divorce?" McDonald asked.

"Shit! Too damn complicated. You got to have a lawyer. You got to know where she's livin'. You need dough. I talked to one lawyer 'bout it a couple years ago, and he wanted two hundred bucks to get started. Two hundred bucks!" Torrance leaned back in his chair with a gallows smile. "I've never had two hundred bucks all at one time in my whole life. Never. So that was that."

"All right," Tony said, straightening the small stack of papers in front of him. He didn't like poking around in Torrance's personal life. That really wasn't their business. "Let's go over both of those nights in detail. The nights of the two murders".

For the next two hours they had Torrance run through his story over and over again. Each time Tony would ask more questions, trying to fill in more facts. McDonald never stopped taking notes, and occasionally interjected a question. Torrance told them how they could locate Lucy Jenks to confirm that she had been with him on the night of January 8th. He also named several of the airmen he was drinking with at Blake's Tavern the night that Laurie McAllister was killed. Torrance's alibis were believable, and, if they could be verified, they would provide a good defense, Tony thought.

It was dark outside by the time they finished. They packed up their papers, told Torrance not to discuss the case with anyone else, including other prisoners, and said they'd be in touch.

Tony was pleased with their first meeting. George Torrance was a tough character, but it didn't look like he had anything to do with the two rapes and murders. Tony was also happy to have Wally McDonald working with him. He could see he was going to be helpful after all.

They stopped for a drink at the Officers' Club after leaving the stockade. Both of them wanted to talk about the case and digest what they'd just learned. Tony called Karen and asked her to join them. By the time she arrived they were on their second round, feeling quite optimistic about the job ahead. They all decided to have lobsters for dinner; flown in live just that afternoon and utterly delicious, besides being a welcome bargain at only $3.95 a person.

Tony and Karen learned a lot about Wally McDonald that evening. His dad owned a successful insurance agency in the St. Louis suburbs. Wally had joined the Air Force Reserves when he was studying at Notre Dame to guarantee that he'd be able to finish school rather than risk being drafted. When he got his J.D. he was automatically promoted to first lieutenant. Both Wally and Patty had worked for his dad until Wally got his orders to report to Lackland Air Force in San Antonio for training in mid-November. Patty stayed on until they learned where his first permanent assignment would be, getting things organized and packed for their eventual assignment.

Wally was a "double domer". He'd not only attended law school in the shadow of the Golden Dome, but had been an undergrad Accounting major there. Wally admitted to being a rabid Irish and St. Louis Cardinals fan. Tony had no problem with the Irish side of that equation, but told Wally he might have irreconcilable differences when it came to the Cards versus the Cubs rivalry. They agreed that the four of them would have to make a trip to Chicago next summer to catch the Cards in one of their games at Wrigley Field. The losers would buy dinner. Tony said they could probably stay at his family's summer home in New Buffalo, Michigan, a ninety minute drive this side of Chicago.

They talked about the Torrance case sporadically. Tony said that Torrance's alibis sounded plausible and Wally tended to agree, even though he had heard from a friend from Georgia that blacks were notorious liars. Tony knew they had to approach the case with the assumption that their client, George Torrance, was innocent. In the meantime, Tony said, he'd be going back through his law school casebook on criminal law, and he suggested that Wally begin reading the *Manual for Courts Martial*.

That same evening Mayor Carl Schroeder was having dinner at his usual corner table in the dining room of the Redwood Lodge. Since his wife passed away last year, Carl had dined there every night. Sheriff Ben Chapman was at the mayor's table in the dining room of the lodge that evening, along with a special guest, Major James Lee Davis, the 379th Bomb Wing's Executive Officer.

The Redwood Lodge was the only real hotel in Oscoda. Carl had bought it and installed his daughter Caroline as manager when her divorce became final. Its twenty guest rooms were usually filled from early June until Labor Day, but in the wintertime only the restaurant and its adjoining bar were kept open; along with Caroline's suite upstairs. She was in her middle thirties and could be attractive when she cared to be, but she avoided social life these days, devoting all her time to running the Lodge.

There were only a handful of people in the restaurant that night, including three locals at the bar. Their quiet conversations were punctuated by the occasional popping of wood in the fireplace or the howl of the wind outside as someone opened the door.

Carl also owned the county's only lumber mill. His father had founded it in 1890, and it was very successful until a disastrous forest fire that swept the Au Sable Valley in 1911. The lumber mill was rebuilt later, but in the meantime the Schroeder family diversified by purchasing large tracts of abandoned land. It was a brilliant long-range investment plan.

Schroeder's Lumber Mill was run now by Carl's son,

Jack, and did a lot of wholesale rough cutting for commercial yards around Bay City, Midland and Saginaw.

At sixty-three, Carl Schroeder had been mayor of Oscoda for twenty years. He was born there and had never left for more than two weeks at a time. Unlike his younger brothers, he was too old to enlist in World War II, and, during the war years Carl expanded his local influence and made considerable money selling the Army the lumber greatly expand the small Army training field outside Oscoda into the bomber base that became Wurtsmith in 1943. He greeted all the county's permanent residents by name and probably was related to a quarter of them.

People in Oscoda and the surrounding countryside relied on Carl Schroeder to keep things running in an or derly fashion. He was more than just the mayor. It was Carl who'd gotten Ben Chapman appointed deputy sheriff when he left Michigan State after the football season his senior year, and couldn't find a job. It was Carl who'd gotten him promoted five years later when Sheriff Miksis retired. And it was Carl who had arranged, through Oscoda's congressman, to again expand Wurtsmith into a major SAC bomber base in the 1950's. He knew that the base would provide an influx of jobs and income for the county, and it did. Constructing it, with its huge hangars and twelve-thousand-foot main runway, took three years. During that period of time and the dozen years that followed, Oscoda boomed.

Wurtsmith was good for Carl Schroeder, too. It was surely no coincidence that most of the land needed for the base's expansions had to be purchased from the Schroeder family.

But Carl was bothered by what had been happening the past few years. More and more Negroes were being assigned to Wurtsmith. A few officers would have been all right, but most of the Negroes coming in now were enlisted men. They were from cities like Chicago and Detroit; coarse and crude. They were not the kind of people you'd want hanging around your place of business, or trying to get a date with your daughter.

Carl was feeling partly responsible for the problem. He could see his town deteriorating. Now his worst nightmare had come true. Peggy Wilton and Laurie McAllister had been raped and murdered by one of those damn Negro airmen. The killer had been caught, thank God! Carl had to make sure the bastard was severely punished. The other Negroes on base had to learn that there would be terrible consequences if they ever bothered any citizen of Oscoda again, particularly a women.

That was why he'd asked Major Davis to join him and Ben Chapman for dinner at the Redwood. Major Davis would be sympathetic, he'd understand the problem. Caroline served them three excellent porterhouse steaks for dinner. Carl saved the aged porterhouses for his special guests. During the course of the meal, he explained his concerns.

Major Davis said very little during dinner, but afterward, over dessert, that changed. He took a sip of his black coffee and put the cup firmly down. "What you want, Mr. Mayor," he said, "is a loud and clear message to every Negro on base: stay as far away as you can from Oscoda and its good citizens. Right?"

"That's it exactly! And there's only one way to accomplish that." Carl poked his fork at Davis as he spoke. "This bastard Torrance has got to be executed. I don't want anything less than the death penalty. Do you understand?"

"Yes, sir," Davis said, taking another sip of his coffee. "I think that's an eminently reasonable penalty for someone who's committed crimes of this nature. I wouldn't be at all surprised if our court martial imposed the death penalty."

"That's not good enough, major," Schroeder said very succinctly. "I want a guarantee. I want *your* guarantee."

Davis leaned back in his chair and looked at the white-haired Mayor for a moment. He paused then nodded. "All right, Mr. Mayor. You've got it."

"There's something I want to add to that," Ben Chapman said, pushing his coffee cup to one side. "It's in the nature of a personal request."

"What is it, Sheriff?" Davis asked.

"I want that bastard castrated before he goes down!"

"Tony, look at this!" Wally McDonald placed an open book on top of the yellow legal pad in Tony's lap. "It's the Uniform Code of Military Justice. Look at Article 25."

As they had been doing every evening since McDonald arrived on base, after they'd grab a quick dinner with Karen at the Officers' Club, they would retire to the Jeffries' apartment or their office to work on the Torrance case. Law books and legal pads were scattered around the couch and coffee table where Tony and Wally were working, while Karen read an Ian Fleming novel and sipped white wine.

"Under the Code, we can insist that the court martial panel include some enlisted men," Wally said, pointing to the book in Tony's lap. "That's a right that any enlisted person has who's charged with a crime in the military. Did you know that?"

"No, I didn't." Tony paused to read Article 25. Wally was right. This put a whole new light on their case. "What do you know?" Tony said, looking up with a smile.

"An enlisted man on the court is going to be much more sympathetic to a fellow enlisted man than an officer's likely to be, don't you think?" Wally asked, stepping back.

"Absolutely! That's a great tactic. We want as many enlisted men on that Court as we can get. Let's prepare a formal demand for the Court to include enlisted personnel, and file it with Breckenridge tomorrow."

"You know, Tony," Wally said, grinning, "I think we're going to do all right for Torrance in this trial."

"So do I." Tony clenched his fist and raised it high in the air. "Tom Donovan, whoever the hell you are, we've got you on the run!"

"Take no prisoners!" Wally shouted in response.

Chapter 7

—ww—

Alex Breckenridge decided to appoint Lieutenant Colonel Lucien Grundig as President of George Torrance's court martial. As the Wing's Chief Personnel Officer, Grundig was under Breckenridge's direct personal command and would be very sensitive to his concerns.

Jimmy Lee Davis had a similar rationale for suggesting the appointment of Major Clark Smithfield to the seven-man court. Smithfield was the Wing's Chief Munitions Officer and also reported directly to Breckenridge. He'd already been passed over once for promotion to Lieutenant Colonel, and a negative evaluation from Breckenridge now would probably end his military career. The Wing Commander thought him an excellent suggestion.

Breckenridge was relaxing in his office with Davis, having their usual after-hours drink and deciding the composition of the court that would try Airman George Torrance.

They decided that the panel should also include some

officers from the flight crews, perhaps one senior man and two younger officers from the same squadron, who would be inclined to follow his lead. They concluded that Lieutenant Colonel Mike Bolte would be an excellent choice. A West Point graduate and a B-52 Command Pilot, he'd risen fast within SAC. He was notorious for demanding the highest standards from everyone and had been ruthless in driving marginal performers out of his squadron - and out of the Air Force. He wouldn't have the remotest sympathy for someone like Torrance.

Major Davis flipped through the pages of the flight duty rosters and came up with two younger officers who he was sure would follow Mike Bolte's lead: Captain Angelo Fanzone, a B-52 co-pilot who'd recently decided to make the Air Force his career, and First Lieutenant John Kopecky, an Electronics Warfare Officer on his first tour of duty. Both men served in Bolte's squadron.

When it was time to honor Jeffries's formal request and name two enlisted men to the Court. Breckenridge and Davis looked at each other and smiled.

"Jimmy, Jeffries has just made the kind of dumb rookie mistake that we anticipated. Let's take advantage of it. Who are the two toughest, meanest sons-of-bitches we have serving as NCO's on this Base?" Breckenridge emptied his glass and reached back to his credenza for the bottle of Jack Daniels. He refilled both their glasses.

"Thank you, Colonel," Davis said, nodding to the Wing Commander and taking a sip of the whiskey. "Colonel, we're blessed with having many men who fit that description serving under us. But if I had to pick just two, I'd name Zeke Longtree and Marcus Jackson. They'd both get a great deal of pleasure in sending someone to their death, legally."

"But Jackson's colored. Mightn't he be inclined to give a little help to a fellow Negra?"

"Just the opposite," Davis said, sipping his whiskey. "He's tough as hell on colored airmen. Punks like Torrance embarrass him. No, I think we can count on Sergeant Jackson to do …" he paused and smiled. "The *right* thing."

"Jimmy, are you bothered by the fact that Jackson was on Pawlowski's original list of suspects?"

"Hell no, colonel. First of all, we *know* that Jackson couldn't have been involved because his pick-up wasn't drivable when the Wilton girl got killed. His name was one of the first that Mitch scratched out. Second, who even knows about that original list besides you, me and Mitch? Maybe one or two of his men, but they're not going to say anything. Finally, we *know* that Torrance is the goddamn killer, so what's the difference?"

Davis' logic was unassailable. Master Sergeant Zeke Longtree and Senior Master Sergeant Marcus Jackson would round off the Court. The orders appointing the seven court members would be issued the next day, February fifteenth.

"Happy Valentine's Day, Airman Torrance," Davis said with a smile as he collected his papers.

"I'll drink to that," Breckenridge responded, raising his glass.

Tony and Karen invited the McDonalds over for dinner Saturday night, rather than dining at the Officers' Club. Patty McDonald had just arrived, and this would be the Jeffries' first chance to meet her. Tony had grown up enjoying thick steaks for special dinners, but he and Karen couldn't afford steaks so a five-pound ham would do just fine. Karen cooked it with brown sugar and sliced pineapples.

Tony's contribution was French onion soup. He took a certain pride in his onion soup; it was always a success. The worst part was slicing up the Bermuda onions. Tonight, as usual, Tony's eyes were tearing so badly that he had to stop slicing several times to rinse them.

Tony and Karen talked a lot about the Torrance case as they worked on dinner. As he scraped the sliced onions into a bowl, Tony said, "I've really got mixed feelings about this case. On the one hand it's very exciting to be working on a murder case, and I'm beginning to feel that Wally and I can do a good job. We're working well as a team. I'm convinced that Torrance isn't guilty, and if we work hard enough we should be able to prove that." Tony dumped the onions into their biggest pan to be sautéed. Wouldn't that be a spectacular way to start a career?"

"It sure would," Karen smiled as she handed him a jar of cranberry sauce. "In the meantime, Clarence Darrow, why don't you open this for me."

Tony gave the jar a couple of good twists and pried open the top. He handed it back to Karen, returning to stir the onions and adding some butter.

"On the other hand," Tony said, getting back to the impending trial. "I'm worried about the responsibility that's been laid on me. When we reported to Wurtsmith, I never imagined that I'd be defending a man's life in a murder trial within a few weeks. Major Cunningham should be defending this case, not me. How could the Air Force have transferred him to Milwaukee at a time like this? I don't understand it at all."

"You'll do just fine," Karen said tearing apart a head of lettuce for the salad. "Remember, you didn't lose a debate your last two years at DePauw. And you won the moot court championship in law school. Besides, didn't Colonel Goldsmith say that you were the best young lawyer he's ever worked with? Think of it as just another moot court case." She smiled, slicing the tomatoes.

"Only bigger," Tony answered. "Much bigger. And with a hell of a lot more at stake."

They were interrupted by a knock at the door. It was the McDonalds. Wally brushed his snow-covered hair back from his eyes as he stepped in, made the introductions and handed Tony a bottle of Lancer's Rosé. Tony was grateful; he knew his one bottle of Chardonnay wouldn't last the evening.

Patty McDonald was blond, blue-eyed, and, at 5'4", a little taller than Karen. She had freckles and a pert turned-up nose. She laughed about making one wrong turn after another on her drive from St. Louis the previous day. Patty was outgoing and pleasant. Tony led them into the living room area of their apartment, opened Wally's Lancer's and poured them each a drink, as they made themselves comfortable and chatted for a few minutes. When Patty offered to help Karen with dinner, Tony welcomed the opportunity to talk to Wally about the case.

The two men began discussing their defense of George Torrance. /Tony had already interviewed the sheriff, examined both crime scenes and initiated back-ground checks on both victims and the defendant. They agreed that the next thing they had to do was to confirm Torrance's two alibis. "That shouldn't be difficult," Tony said, "because Torrance has been very specific about where he'd been and whom he'd been with the night of both murders." They divided up the responsibilities. Tony would find and talk to Torrance's girlfriend, Lucy Jenks in Saginaw, to confirm her alibi for the night of the first killing, while Wally would check out Blake's Tavern for witnesses to his presence there early on January 29th.

Dinner was a great success, especially Tony's soup. The hearty shot of sherry that he added just before serving it gave the soup some extra panache. They talked about their experiences before the Air Force, their favorite sports teams and the places they'd been. As they finished dessert and the last of the Chardonnay by candlelight, Tony realized how fortunate he and Karen were to have these new friends. Without them, the bleak terrain and endless snow could make serving at Wurtsmith a grim and lonely experience.

"To new, dear friends," Tony said, raising his glass. "And to the great adventures ahead of us."

Tony had trouble locating Lucy Jenks, even with Torrance's directions; which weren't as clear as they could have been. She lived in Saginaw, about an hour-and-a-half's drive south of Oscoda and shared an apartment with two other young women. It was a walk-up flat over a small restaurant, the Esquire, in the old downtown section. After he found her late that morning they met to talk over coffee in one of the restaurant's booths. She already knew about the charges from visiting Torrance in the brig, and suspected that Tony would be coming to talk to her.

Tony guessed that she hadn't eaten yet that day and decided the Esquire would be a good spot to have lunch, even though it was a bit early, and asked Lucy if she'd care to join him. She said she'd be happy to, since she hadn't had any breakfast. They each ordered a barbecue pork sandwich, the special of the day.

Lucy was an attractive woman, on the thin side, with dark ebony skin and short, curly black hair. She was wearing a tight tan sweater and jeans and, Tony noticed, no bra. She had a nice figure. Tony guessed that she was about twenty or twenty-one. Her family was originally from Mississippi. They'd moved to Saginaw about ten years ago when her father got a job in the Dow Chemical plant in Midland, about twenty miles away. Negroes weren't welcome in Midland, so they lived in Saginaw and her father drove to work every day. He died a year ago from some sort of lung disease, and her mother moved back south. Lucy decided to stay in Saginaw because that was where all her friends were. She had been having a hard time making a go of it ever since, and right now didn't have a job.

"I've known George about six months," Lucy said. "A friend of mine introduced us last summer; we've been seeing each other ever since. George has been good to me. He even gave me a car so that I can drive up and visit him when he can't get off base."

"A car! That's a pretty nice gift."

"Well, not a *new* car, Cap'n Jeffries," she smiled. "It's an old Chevy. But it's still a car."

Tony hesitated before he asked his next question. "Did you know that he has a wife?" It was awkward, but he had to ask it.

"Sure I did," she answered with a shrug. "George told me all about her. He tol' me they're gettin' divorced." She paused and smiled at Tony, adding, "But men say things like that, don't they, when they're trying to get what they want."

Tony took a sip of his coffee. "What I need to know, Lucy," he asked, "is whether you were with George on the night of January eighth. If you were, and we can corroborate that, it'll go a long way toward getting George out of this jam."

"Cap'n Jeffries," she said, leaning forward and looking directly at Tony, "I drove up to Wurtsmith early that evenin' and spent the night with George. We was in his room in the barracks the whole time." Her eyes glistened with moisture, and she looked down.

She leaned back and, after a moment, looked up at him. Her eyes were still moist. "Cap'n, you may not know this, and you may not even care, but George is a good, decent man. I know him better'n anybody else in this whole world, and I can tell you that there ain't no way that George would kill anybody. No way!"

Tony nodded silently. For a moment neither of them spoke. Tony looked down at the black coffee that he was swirling in his cup, then back up at Lucy. He knew that she was telling him the truth. George Torrance had been with her in the barracks when the first murder occurred.

Lucy broke the silence by saying that she would testify to that in court if Jeffries wanted her to. Tony said that would be very important, and asked if there was anyone else who could confirm that she was with George that night. She said she didn't think there was.

Before he left, Tony got a description of Lucy's car. It was a '58 red Chevy two-door with Michigan license plate BB-126. He said that maybe someone else could recall seeing that car parked on base that night. He would check into that.

Tony thanked Lucy for her time and said that he'd keep her advised. She was a very credible witness, and her testimony would be crucial to George Torrance's defense.

Wally McDonald's attempt to verify Torrance's alibi at Blake's Tavern didn't go as well. Blake's was a dirty, dimly-lit saloon on River Road, southwest of the base. Wally went there late the same afternoon that Tony searched out Lucy Jenks in Saginaw and tried to talk to a few of the bar's regulars, men Torrance said he was drinking with that night. They all knew Torrance, but none of them wanted to talk about the case and some could recall he'd been there early on the morning of January 29th, the night that Laurie McAllister was murdered but weren't sure when he came or left.

He said he'd return later to talk to some of the other regulars who had been with Torrance that night. Wally especially wanted to interview the other bartender, a black airman named Ash who he missed on his first visit. Torrance said that Ash would definitely verify that he was there until about 4 or 5:00 a.m. on the 29th.

Wally was sure that if he talked to enough people he'd find someone who could back up George Torrance's alibi.

Lieutenant Colonel Lucien Grundig surveyed the large conference room in the Headquarters Building where the court martial would be conducted. The room was about fifty feet square, with wood-paneled walls on three sides and a large window on the fourth, overlooking the Base's main runway. Stacks of folding steel chairs leaned up against one wall next to a gurney holding a pile of folding conference tables.

As one of the senior officers on base, working directly under Colonel Breckenridge's command, Lucien Grundig had discussed the case several times privately with the wing commander, and knew exactly what Breckenridge expected from the Torrance court martial and what his job was. He had no intention of letting the Commander down.

"How's the room going to be set up for the trial, Major?" Grundig asked Jimmy Lee Davis.

"Well, sir, that depends on whether we follow the traditional format of conducting trials, or the new, optional one being recommended by the Secretary of Defense's office."

"What's the difference?"

"Under the traditional method, as you probably know, the court sits at a long table at the head of the room with the senior officer, in the center, presiding. The Law Officer, who'll be Colonel Goldsmith, sits to the side and only rules on issues of law that arise. Under the new format the Law Officer presides, like a Judge, and the members of the court sit to the side, like a jury. That's what's being recommended, but it won't be required until next year."

"And who makes the decision as to which format will be used?"

"The senior officer on the court, sir."

"That would be me, I take it."

"Yes, sir, Colonel."

"In that case, let's follow the traditional format," Grundig answered. "I'll preside over this Court Martial."

"Fine, sir, we'll set up the room that way."

———*wm*———

A sleek T-33 broke out of the high gray clouds, circled the base in a broad 360-degree sweep, landed and rolled up the twelve-thousand-foot runway to the hangar area. When the plane came to a stop, the canopy flipped back on its hinge and the officer in the rear seat dropped to the ground. He opened the travel pod attached to the plane's underbelly, pulled out his duffel bag, and flipped the pod shut.

Captain Tom Donovan had arrived at Wurtsmith Air Force Base.

He waved and thanked his friend for the ride, zipped up his leather jacket, picked up his bag and strode off the tarmac. The seven-hundred mile flight from Omaha had taken a little more than an hour.

A car was waiting for him. The driver took him directly to the wing headquarters building, where he met Colonel Breckenridge, Major Davis and the Staff Judge Advocate, Lieutenant Colonel Mel Goldsmith. They reviewed the Torrance case file that had been sent to Donovan earlier, outlined the composition of the court, and handed him the original files on the two rapes and murders. He gave the documents a quick browse and asked a couple of questions. Donovan had already reviewed his copy of the files intensely in the two weeks since he'd received them and felt that he already had a good handle on the prosecutor's evidence and witnesses. There seemed to be ample evidence to convict on all of the counts. "Is there somewhere I can organize this material and set up a war room?" he asked and Davis quickly found him an empty nearby office.

An hour later, Donovan asked to meet Special Agent Pawlowski and was taken to his office. It was time to meet his witnesses, up close and personal. He knew that his evidence was only as good as the witnesses who would present it, and he was pleased to find that Pawlowski and his men were real pros. They weren't likely to make mistakes either collecting the evidence or in presenting it at trial.

Finally, he stopped at the Legal Office. He wanted to size up the defense counsel, Captain Jeffries. Donovan knew most of the JAG officers in SAC, but he'd never meet Tony Jeffries. He was disappointed that Bob Cunningham wasn't handling the defense. He'd tried a case opposite him a few years ago; and, even though Donovan won, he came away with a great deal of respect for Cunningham's ability as a trial lawyer. Nothing makes a victory more satisfying than beating a tough opponent.

Jeffries seemed awfully young to be a Captain, Donovan thought when they met. Still, looks can be deceiving. He knew that somebody must have thought that Jeffries was a damn good lawyer, or he wouldn't be defending a case like this.

The trial was scheduled to begin in three days, February 21st. When it did, Donovan knew that he'd see just how good this Captain Jeffries was.

———*um*———

"Tony, there's nothing here, nothing." Wally tossed Torrance's Air Force file on Tony's desk and dropped into one of the straight-backed chairs facing it. "At least, nothing that would be the slightest help to us. I've gone through every line, every word, followed up on every name mentioned, and, believe me, there's nothing here that we'd want to even touch in court."

"Well, that's too bad," Tony responded, taking off his wire-rim glasses and rubbing his eyes. He'd been working on trial preparation material all day. "I was hoping that you'd find something – anything – that we could use in our favor in the trial. But you say there's nothing there?"

"Nothing! Absolutely nothing!"

"By the way," Tony added after a pause, looking Wally in the eye, "I met our opponent, Captain Donovan today. He just arrived and stopped by to introduce himself."

"And…"

"And, he's going to be a tough son-of-a-bitch in trial," Tony answered slowly. "One *tough* son-of-a-bitch."

Chapter 8

—*mm*—

66"The Court will come to order!"
Lieutenant Colonel Lucien Grundig banged his gavel and the room hushed. "Are you ready to proceed, gentlemen?" he asked.

"Ready for the Prosecution," Captain Tom Donovan rose and answered with an almost imperceptible swagger.

Colonel Grundig looked to Tony Jeffries.

"Ready for the Defense," his chair squeaking loudly as he pushed it back. He tried, without success, to sound as confident as Donovan appeared. Tony's palms were wet, and he could feel the sweat running down the middle of his back. He hoped it didn't show through his uniform jacket.

The Court Martial of Airman Second Class George Torrance had begun.

The seven-man Court sat at a long table at one end of the large conference room, with curtained windows and the flags of the United States and the Strategic Air

Command furled and crossed behind them. To their left, at a small separate table, was the Law Officer, Lieutenant Colonel Mel Goldsmith, ready to rule on any questions of law that arose.

Colonel Grundig sat in the center of the court's long table. To his right were Major Clark Smithfield, Captain Angelo Fanzone and Master Sergeant Zeke Longtree. To his left were Lieutenant Colonel Michael Bolte, First Lieutenant John Kopecky and Senior Master Sergeant Marcus Jackson. All had copies of the charges against Torrance in front of them, and all except for Major Smithfield, whom he once had met briefly, were total strangers to Tony.

In front of the court, on the opposite side from the Law Officer were the witnesses' chair and the court reporter, Ruth Olmsted. She was not only the Legal Office's receptionist, but also the only certified court reporter in the county. Farther in front of the court, angled slightly inward, were the defense and prosecution tables. Tony Jeffries sat between Wally McDonald and George Torrance at one table. Piles of paper and a dozen law books filled all the available space they had. Captain Tom Donovan sat at the other table by himself. He had a small stack of perhaps a dozen papers in front of him, the *Manual for Courts Martial* to one side, and looked completely at ease.

The room was filled with about a hundred people, using every folding chair that had been set up. The trial had generated a great deal of interest. Ashtrays were on the floor beside every third seat. Two armed air policemen sat in the front row directly behind the defense table.

This was the first General Court Martial held at Wurtsmith in five years and the first murder case ever tried in Iosco County. The *Iosco County* News featured a front page story about the trial in its weekly edition that had been published two days earlier. It was also being covered by *The Detroit Free Press*. Civilian spectators had to obtain passes to attend the trial, and the air policemen at the gate were careful not to admit anyone without proper I.D. or anyone they recalled from the anti-war protestors. Curious airmen and officers filled the rest of the seats, stood along the back wall, and spilled out into the hall. The quiet buzz of conversation so prevalent earlier had vanished and the only sounds that broke the silence were occasional coughs.

"Will the Prosecutor please read the charges," Lieutenant Colonel Grundig intoned, following the format that Mel Goldsmith had furnished.

Tom Donovan rose, picked up a single piece of paper from his desk, and slowly read the formal charges, pausing to emphasize the key words and phrases. "The United States of America charges Airman Second Class George Torrance with *willfully* murdering Peggy Wilton and Laurie McAllister in violation of Article 118 of the Uniform Code of Military Justice. He is also separately charged under Article 120 with *aggravated* rape of both women. There are *four* counts." He paused to catch the eye of every man on the Court, before slowly sitting down.

"Does the defendant understand the nature of the charges against him?" Grundig asked.

"He does, sir." Jeffries replied.

"And how does the defendant plead?"

"The defendant pleads not guilty to all charges." The reporters in the crowd began taking notes.

"Captain Jeffries," Grundig said, slowly removing his glasses, "I'd prefer to have the defendant himself respond to the charges."

Torrance slowly stood up and glanced at Tony, who nodded. "Not guilty, sir," he quietly said.

"All right, we will proceed. Are there any preliminary motions by either side?"

"Yes there are, sir," Tony said, rising. "The defense moves for the exclusion of all witnesses from the trial except when they are being called to testify."

Colonel Grundig turned to the Law Officer. Mel Goldsmith nodded and said, "The motion is in order and will be granted. All parties who expect to be called as witnesses will leave and wait in the hallway until they are called."

Well, that's something that worked, Tony said to himself, as he watched a half-dozen people stand and leave. He had read about Motions to Exclude Witnesses the previous night.

George Torrance's eyes moved up and down the court as the witnesses left the room. "I know some of these men," he said quietly to his lawyers. "They're mean motherfuckers."

Grundig leaned back, lit his pipe, and laid his leather tobacco pouch on the table in front of him. Mel Goldsmith, Captain Fanzone and a dozen others in the room followed Grundig's lead, and also lit up. Every man on the court had his own ashtray in front of him, as did Goldsmith.

It was time for the prosecution's opening statement. Tom Donovan strode around his table to stand in front of the court. He wasn't carrying any notes. That surprised Tony. Donovan began in a conversational tone, as if he were discussing the two murders privately with good friends.

"A horrible thing has occurred here," he said. "Horrible, not only to the victims and their families, but to the whole Oscoda community and the very integrity of the United States Air Force. This is an old, quiet community. Most of the families here go back a hundred years or more. They have solid, old-fashioned values. They invited the Air Force here, opening their doors in welcome. And look what happened! One of our men savagely raped and murdered two of their daughters! The shame of it extends to all of us," he said walking back and forth before the court, looking each man in the eye. "We," he said forcefully, "*We* are responsible for atoning for this horror that we have inflicted upon them."

As he spoke Donovan felt his rapport with the members of the Court grow, and he steadily became more forceful.

"Fortunately," he said, "the murderer has been caught. The people of Oscoda no longer have to fear that he's lurking somewhere in the shadows." His voice rose as he turned and pointed at the defendant. *"That man is Airman George Torrance!"* His accusing finger had the impact of a gun. Torrance cowered noticeably.

"The prosecution will prove beyond any reasonable doubt that George Torrance was the rapist and killer," Donovan said. "Not only were there eyewitnesses who saw him at the scene of the first crime, but Torrance was careless enough to leave an item of his at the scene of the second murder." Tony caught his breath at that.

"At the conclusion of this trial," Donovan continued, "there will be no doubt in anyone's mind that George Torrance is guilty of all the crimes charged."

Tony and Wally looked at each other.

"Do they have that kind of evidence?" McDonald whispered.

"I guess they do. This is worse than I thought. In law school they talked about discovery and depositions and things like that. Nobody ever mentioned that in courts martial there is no discovery. None!" Tony paused, turned to Torrance. "What are they talking about, George? Don't bullshit me!"

"Nothin' man," Torrance said, shaking his head back and forth. "He's jus' jivin' you."

"I don't think so," Tony answered quietly. "I think he's got something of yours. And I think he's got someone who's identified you."

Torrance just shrugged, turning back toward the court as Tom Donovan completed his opening statement.

Donovan concluded by telling the court that at the end of the trial the prosecution would be asking for the imposition of the death penalty. He was sure they would agree that execution was the only penalty that fit crimes of this heinous nature.

That caught George Torrance's attention. He sat up in his chair and blinked several times as he watched Donovan walk back to the prosecutor's table and sit down. He turned as though to say something to Tony but stopped and leaned back.

Tony's opening statement was built around the fact that the defendant had airtight alibis for both nights, which he briefly reviewed, "As we will prove during the trial," Tony said, looking at each member of the court, "the murderer couldn't have been Airman Torrance. It had to have been somebody else; perhaps two different killers. It's been bad enough that two women have suffered terrible deaths," Tony said, "but the members of the court shouldn't compound that tragedy by condemning an innocent man on a few strands of circumstantial evidence, which is the best that can be said for the prosecution's case." Glancing down at his notes, he continued, "Let me remind you that the prosecution has the burden of proving the defendant's guilt beyond a reasonable doubt. That is a burden," he said raising his voice, "that will be impossible for the prosecutor to carry in this case, because it simply isn't true."

Tony felt uneasy as he returned to the defense table. He hadn't said enough. He hadn't responded adequately to all the points Donovan had made.

"Not bad." Wally whispered as Tony sat down.

"I don't know. I don't feel good about this. I think they've got a lot more on Torrance than we realize."

George Torrance took no part in the conversation; glancing their way only briefly. It was as though someone else's life was being discussed.

The prosecution's first witness was the Iosco County Medical Examiner, Dr. James Cox. He was a slight man in his late fifties with thin gray hair and wire-rim bifocals. He testified that he graduated from the University of Michigan School of Medicine and had interned at Michael Reese Hospital in Chicago. He served as a surgeon with the Army during the War, rising to the rank of Major. After the War he took two years of postgraduate training under the GI Bill, and moved to Tawas City, the County Seat, where he got the job of medical examiner. His wife's family was from that area. He said that he maintained a private medical practice on the side.

He testified about the details of both murders, accentuating his testimony with large color photographs of both victims. They were graphic and brutal, showing both women with their throats slit. Dr. Cox testified that their autopsies, which he had with him, confirmed that both women had also been raped.

"Dr. Cox, did the autopsies of the two victims disclose any evidence that would have any bearing on the identity of the killer or killers?" Donovan asked.

"Yes. Both autopsies revealed evidence of that

nature," the medical examiner answered.

"Would you tell us what you found, please?" Donovan stepped back as he asked the question. The court's full attention was now focused on the witness.

"Certainly. First of all, we found foreign pubic hairs on both victims' bodies. Human hair has some distinctive characteristics from person to person, even pubic hair. By examining the hairs we found on both women we concluded that they had probably come from the same man."

"In each case, doctor, was it your conclusion that the rapes occurred at approximately the same time as the victims were murdered?" Donovan asked.

"Yes; no question about it."

"So, it's your opinion that both women were murdered by the same man?"

"Objection!" Tony declared, raising from his chair. "Leading question."

"Denied," Goldsmith answered curtly. "The witness will answer the question."

"The question," Donovan repeated, "is whether it is your professional opinion that both women were raped and murdered by the same man?"

"That certainly appears to be the case."

Dr. Cox's answers were crisp and confident. He gave the impression of being a competent and thorough professional. Tony wondered what he could possibly ask him on cross-examination.

"What else did you find, doctor, relating to the identity of the killer?"

Tony immediately noticed that Donovan had dropped the phrase "or killers" from his question.

"Both women had skin fragments under their finger-nails," the Medical Examiner answered. "They both gave their assailant some pretty good scratches. On examining those skin fragments, and their pigmentation, we concluded that the assailant in both cases was a Negro."

"A Negro?" Donovan asked.

"Yes, a Negro."

"Shee-it," George Torrance muttered under his breath. Tony turned to him. "They's doin' a real job on me, Cap'n," he said, shaking his head.

The Medical Examiner was still testifying. "We also concluded that the killer was almost certainly left-hand-ed," he said.

"Why do you say that, doctor?" Donovan was serving his witness easy lobs.

"Because the stab wounds on both victims were in front and on their right sides. Besides their slit throats, of course," the witness corrected himself. "No stab wounds were on the left side of either victim's body. Since both victims had multiple cuts on their right hands, that indicates that the attacker was holding the knife in his left hand as he faced them, and was therefore left-handed."

"I see," Donovan nodded and paused a moment. "Did you find anything else, doctor?" he asked.

"Yes, we did," the Medical Examiner answered. "From our analysis of the skin fragments, the roots of the pubic hairs found on both victims, and the fresh blood stains found at Miss McAllister's house, we concluded that the killer has type A blood."

"Did Miss McAllister have type A blood?"

"No, she didn't." Dr. Cox glanced down at Laurie McAllister's autopsy. "She had O negative blood."

"So is it your professional medical opinion, Dr. Cox, that both women were killed by the same person, and that the killer was a left-handed male Negro with type A blood?"

"Yes it is."

Several men on the court leaned forward at that point and began making notes on the yellow pads that were at each place. The reporters in the first row of the audience had never stopped writing.

Donovan picked a thin manila folder off his table and walked over to the witness.

"Dr. Cox," he said, handing the folder to the Medical Examiner. "These are the official Air Force medical records of Airman George Torrance. I've had them authenticated and marked as Exhibit A for the prosecution. I'd like you to look at them and tell us whether Airman Torrance is left-handed or right-handed."

Dr. Cox opened the folder and thumbed through it for a moment.

"He's left-handed," he said finally.

"And would you tell us Airman Torrance's blood type, doctor."

"Type A."

"So would you conclude, doctor, that the killer in both

cases was a left-handed male Negro, with Type A blood, such as Airman George Torrance?"

"Yes, I would."

"Thank you, doctor." Donovan turned to the defense table, gave Jeffries a nod and a slight smile, adding, "Your witness, counsel."

—————

Jeffries tried in cross-examination to somehow break down Dr. Cox's testimony. After an hour, he was exhausted as well as frustrated. All he could accomplish was to obtain an acknowledgment that 41 percent of the public has Type A blood. He also conceded that as Medical Examiner, rather than County Coroner, his primary work was as a private general practitioner, and that he was called upon to act as Medical Examiner by the Court only once or twice a month. He had no particular training in forensic pathology although he felt fully qualified to testify in that area.

On redirect examination, Donovan only asked Dr. Cox one question. "Doctor, what percentage of the population has Type A blood as well as being left-handed?"

"Based on the research we've reviewed, only five percent of people had both those two characteristics."

Tony's shoulders sagged as he leaned back in his chair.

The medical examiner's last answer brought a wave of murmurs from the audience. Wally glanced back, and leaned over to Tony. "Jesus Christ. Everybody here regards us as the bad guys. But this is all circumstantial. None of it really ties Torrance to either murder."

"I know," Tony said quietly. "But it sure as hell doesn't look good."

At the conclusion of Dr. Cox's testimony, his autopsies of the two victims and George Torrance's Air Force medical records were admitted into evidence.

After a break for lunch, the afternoon was devoted to identifying and resolving the admissibility of numerous photographs of both murder scenes. The Medical Examiner's office as well as the OSI had taken full sets of color photos. Both women, mutilated and nude, were shown from various angles, where they were found, as well as on the Medical Examiner's slabs. Close-ups of every wound, including the knife thrust into Laurie McAllister's groin, were marked and tendered as prosecution exhibits. The pictures were so inflammatory that Jeffries tried to keep out as many as he could. Eventually, however, one-by-one, they were all admitted into evidence.

At four-thirty Colonel Grundig gaveled the proceedings to a close. "The trial will resume at nine tomorrow morning,: he said, "and I remind everyone that some members of the court had important Air Force administrative duties to deal with, besides this Court Martial." Everyone rose and began milling around the courtroom to leave.

Tony packed up his briefcase. He wasn't comfortable about the way the trial's first day had gone. Behind him,

McDonald and Torrance were engaged in a quiet but intense discussion. The two air policemen assigned to guard the defendant were discreetly standing a few yards away, hands on their sidearms.

"Tony, Torrance wants to talk to you," Wally whispered as he came to Jeffries' side. He looked upset.

"What is it?" Tony motioned Torrance toward him.

George Torrance ambled over, exhaling a stream of smoke. When he got to Tony he dropped his cigarette on the tile floor and slowly ground it out.

"Cap'n Jeffries," he said, looking down at his lawyer. "I wanna make a deal. I wanna plea."

"What?" Tony was stunned.

"Yeah. If they drop this bullshit about the death penalty and life, maybe we can make a deal." Torrance looked at him through his tough street-wise eyes, adding, "Maybe I'll plead guilty if we can make a deal for something like twenty. Good behavior would end up makin' that six or seven."

"Damn," Tony said aloud. He shook his head and stared at Torrance.

"That means you're guilty, doesn't it?"

"Fuck no, I didn't kill *nobody*. It means that I know this whole damn court is wired, and they're going to burn me or give me life, no matter what you guys do. The only fuckin' way I'm gonna survive is by a plea. Do you understan' that?"

"That's not right, George," Tony said. "Wally and I think we've got a decent shot at winning this trial. If you're not guilty, I don't want any part of a plea bargain that might put you away for the next twenty years. Do you realize how long twenty years is, George?"

"Don't jive me, man. I know what's goin' on round here. I wanna make the deal."

"We're his lawyers, Tony." Wally said quietly. "If that's what he wants, we're obligated to see if a deal can be made."

Torrance tapped himself on the chest. "That's right. I'm the damn client."

"All right," Tony hesitated. "Let me talk to Donovan."

He took a deep breath, and walked across the courtroom to the prosecutor's table, where Tom Donovan was packing his trial bag. Tony wasn't sure how to handle this.

"Tom, let me ask you something," Tony said quietly. "We've never discussed plea bargains in this case, and maybe we should. My client maintains that he's not guilty, and all you've got is a lot of circumstantial evidence, but if you have any proposal you'd like to make, I'd be duty bound to present it to him."

Donovan looked at Tony for a moment before responding. There was a trace of a smile at the corner of his mouth.

"There's not going to be any plea bargaining, Jeffries," he said. "I don't think that this is a case where a plea bargain would be appropriate."

"Now wait a minute," Tony answered. "The evidence against Torrance is all circumstantial. Your case isn't open-and-shut by any means. It seems to me that this is precisely the kind of case where a plea bargain might be advantageous to both sides."

"Maybe," Donovan smiled as he snapped shut his initialed black leather trial bag. "But you haven't seen all our evidence yet." His smile hardened. "There's another factor too." He paused, "This isn't the first time that George Torrance has killed someone."

Tony's back stiffened. "What do you mean?"

"Back in Macon, Georgia, there was an unsolved rape and murder of one of the cheerleaders at the high school. A white girl. The police couldn't prove it, but they were convinced that George Torrance was the man. He had a real thing about that girl, but she wouldn't give him the time of day. His friends gave him a pretty good alibi the night she was killed, but the police were sure that he did it. Seems as though a knife was used in that killing too. That doesn't appear in his Air Force record, and he was never formally charged, so that won't show up in any other records either. But I don't have any doubt about its truth." Tom Donovan slipped his arms into his heavy winter coat and began buttoning it up.

"The upshot," Donovan continued, turning around, "was that Torrance was told to join the military and get out of town, or some local folks might take the law into their own hands. So he joined the Air Force, and now we have him. Or rather, *you* have him." He gave Tony a slight nod and a smile.

"That's not admissible evidence!" Tony exclaimed.

"He wasn't convicted of anything. You can't use that in court!"

"Oh, I know that, Jeffries. And I don't intend to. But it explains why there isn't going to be any plea bargaining in this case. The good guys have some catching up to do, and I think it's time for Airman George Torrance to meet his Maker."

Chapter 9

———*mm*———

"The prosecution calls as its next witness Major Mitchell Pawlowski." Tom Donovan's confident voice filling the room marked the opening volley of the trial's second day, Wednesday, February 22nd.

A buzz of whispers arose as Pawlowski strode in with a military bearing rarely seen and took the witness chair dressed, as always, in civilian clothes. Until he was announced and called as a witness almost no one present was aware of his military status, much less his rank.

After being sworn in and identified as the Commander of Wurtsmith's Office of Special Investigations, Pawlowski was asked to relate to the Court the details of his investigation into the murder of Peggy Wilton.

He testified that his men had interviewed hundreds of people, both on and off base trying to find someone who might have seen something unusual the night Peggy Wilton was abducted, particularly around the Officers' Club. They'd finally found a young couple who'd been parked on a back road just outside the fence, probably necking; said they saw a man driving away from the Club a little after nine o'clock that night.

"Did you personally interview that couple?" Tom Donovan asked.

"Yes, I did."

"For the record, what are their names?"

"The young man's name is Bill Carlson, and the young woman's name is Brenda Wendt. They're both residents of Oscoda; seniors at Oscoda Consolidated High School. Nice kids."

"After your interview with Mr. Carlson and Miss Wendt, did you reach a conclusion that Peggy Wilton's killer fit a particular description, and was driving any particular type of vehicle?"

"Yes, I did."

"Wait a minute. Objection!" Tony Jeffries was on his feet. "That's hearsay. This witness can't testify as to what the other people saw."

"Counsel, I didn't ask Mr. Pawlowski what the young couple saw or said to him," Donovan answered, turning only halfway toward Tony. "Rather, the question I asked was what conclusions had *Major Pawlowski* reached after talking to them. That's totally different."

"The law is clear on that. The objection is denied," Colonel Goldsmith ruled. "The witness may answer the question."

Donovan nodded to Mitch Pawlowski.

"I concluded that we were looking for a male Negro

driving a Ford pickup with a camper in back."

At the far end of the court's table, Master Sergeant Marcus Jackson visibly flinched. He fit that description.

Mitch Pawlowski told the court that his office had checked the Base Vehicle Registration records. After eliminating the owners of vehicles that were known to be inoperable or out of the immediate area, they came up with a list of five possible suspects, whom he named. When the second murder occurred about three weeks later, he concluded that it was almost certainly committed by the same man. On checking, they found that four of the five possible suspects were gone that night. Two were in the air with the Wing over the Arctic Circle, two others were at the recovery Base in Alpena, an hour's drive away, only one was on base that night. *Airman George Torrance*. Pawlowski turned from the court and looked directly at the defendant as he said his name.

"Major Pawlowski, have you reviewed the medical records of the five possible suspects to determine their blood types?" Donovan picked up a stack of medical records that had been lying on the table in front of him as he asked the question.

"Yes, I have." Pawlowski nodded as he answered.

"Are these the records you examined?" Donovan handed the folders to Pawlowski, who briefly thumbed through them.

"Yes, they are."

"How many of the five suspects have Type A blood?"

"Two. Airman Torrance and Staff Sergeant Nance."

"Major," Donovan asked, "where was Staff Sergeant Nance the night that Laurie McAllister was murdered?"

"He was in a B-52 at fifty thousand feet over Hudson Bay, flying north." The whispered comments in the courtroom behind Tony began again. At the court's table, Lieutenant Kopecky leaned forward and began writing.

"So, Major Pawlowski," Donovan continued, "Is it your testimony that Airman George Torrance is the only one of the five suspects from the Wilton killing who was even in the Oscoda area on the night of the McAllister killing, and who has Type A blood."

"Yes, that's exactly what I'm saying."

"Major, you've reviewed the medical files of the five men on your suspect list. How many of them are left-handed?"

Tony rose to object, hesitated, and sat back down.

"Only one," Pawlowski said, ignoring Tony, looking directly at the court.

"And who would that be, Major?" Donovan asked.

"Airman Second Class George Torrance."

"Thank you, Major Pawlowski," Tom Donovan said as he took the folders back.

"He's killing us!" Tony whispered to Wally.

"Nice choice of words, Tony. Is our client still saying that he's innocent?"

"He hasn't said anything for a long time."

Donovan had Pawlowski describe his investigation into the murder of Laurie McAllister. Pawlowski explained in detail how he searched her house. It was only after several hours, he said, that he finally found some evidence that he thought was relevant. It had been missed in the initial search.

"What did you find, Major?"

"I found a man's wristwatch," Mitch Pawlowski said. "It was behind one of the chairs in the living room. The band was covered with bright turquoise stones and had a broken clasp, as though it had been torn off in a fight. The time was stopped at two-forty."

"Do you recall at what time the Coroner concluded that Laurie McAllister died?" Donovan asked.

"Objection." Tony said, rising to his feet, Dr. Cox has admitted under oath that he is a part-time medical examiner, not an official coroner."

"Sustained." Goldsmith quickly responded. "Please refer to that witness as a medical examiner, not a coroner."

"Let me rephrase the question," Donovan retorted. "At what time did the medical examiner conclude that Laurie McAllister died?"

"Between two and three in the morning."

"So the watch you found would be consistent with one that could have been torn off the killer's wrist and smashed in Laurie McAllister's desperate fight for her life that night, is that true?"

"Yes, it definitely is."

Tony internally winced. He knew he should have objected as Wally glanced at him.

"Apart from the turquoise stones on the band, is there anything distinctive about that watch?" Donovan asked.

"Yes, it's engraved 'G.T.' on the back." Pawlowski replied.

Tony sighed and sat back. He felt the energy flowing out of him. *This* is what Donovan had. It was devastating evidence. Several of the court members exchanged whispered comments with their neighbors, who nodded in response. One of the reporters in the first row fished into his pocket for some change, got up and quickly walked out. His coat, still over the back of his chair, was a sign that he would return.

"Did you determine whether Miss McAllister had any male friends or relatives with the initials G.T.?" Donovan asked. He was twisting the knife now.

"Yes. I interviewed eleven close friends and relatives of the deceased, and none of them had heard of or knew anyone with those initials."

"Is this that watch, Major Pawlowski?" Donovan held up a timepiece with an exhibit tag hanging from it.

"Yes, it is, the tag has my initials on it, along with the date on which I found it."

"Thank you." Donovan placed the watch on his table, among his other exhibits. Turning to the Court, he commented that he would formally introduce the watch with several other items as a series of exhibits later in the case.

Colonel Grundig announced an hour's recess for lunch, and that they would reconvene at one o'clock. He banged his gavel and everyone rose and began donning coats and filing out. Major James Lee Davis, who had been observing from the front row, worked his way through the crowd and congratulated Tom Donovan on how well he was doing. George Torrance stepped away from the two lawyers to talk to a black airman in the audience, his two AP guards close behind him.

"I don't feel much like eating, Wally," Tony said quietly. "I feel like I've been mugged."

"Come on, you've got to get something in your stomach. We've got a long afternoon ahead of us."

"I know and that doesn't make me feel any better."

It got worse for them after lunch. Mitch Pawlowski continued his testimony and said that he had interviewed Airman Torrance just after his arrest. Torrance had alibis for the nights of each of the murders. He was allegedly with his girlfriend, Lucy Jenks, on Base the first night, and with a group of airmen at Blake's Tavern the second. Neither alibi could be substantiated. It was his personal conclusion, he testified, that both were highly questionable.

It was time for Tony to cross-examine Mitch Pawlowski. Tony stood and decided to ask his questions from the defense table.

"Major," he began, "I understand that all of your analyses of possible suspects are based on the premise that the killer of Peggy Wilton was driving a Ford pickup with a camper on the night of January 8th, is that correct?"

"That's right. I'm confident that he was."

"I know you're confident," Tony responded with a smile to the witness. "But if, somehow, the killer was driving some other type of vehicle that night, perhaps a different make of pickup, there'd be a whole new group of possible suspects, wouldn't there?"

"Well, sure," Pawlowski answered. "But we *know* he was driving a Ford pickup."

"That premise is crucial to your analysis, isn't it?" Tony asked.

"Absolutely. We also know that it's true."

"Thank you," Tony said as he sat down. It wasn't much of a point, but Tony knew that right now it was all that he could get from Pawlowski. He planned to follow up on that line of questioning later.

Donovan's next witness identified himself as Airman First Class Eugene Ash. He was neatly dressed in his Air Force blues and began by stating that he was the regular night bartender at Blake's Tavern.

"This is the son-of-a-bitch who's been ducking me for over a week!" Wally whispered to Tony as Ash was sworn in.

"I think we're about to find out why."

Airman Ash testified that he had been working nights at Blake's for about a year. He knew George Torrance well and identified him in the courtroom. He said that Torrance was one of a regular crowd of Airmen who worked the second shift on base, and who showed up at the bar about midnight on most nights. Torrance showed up earlier on nights when he wasn't working; but either way, he was there just about every night.

In response to Donovan's questions Ash testified that Torrance wasn't there the night Laurie McAllister was killed, early morning on January 29th. He remembered that because it was the only night in weeks that Torrance hadn't been there. He knew the regulars and noticed when they weren't there, especially in Torrance's case, since he had promised to stop by and pay his bar bill that night.

Tony leaned over and tapped his client's arm. "What about that, George?"

"That's bullshit, man," Torrance said under his breath. "I was there!"

Tony didn't believe Torrance. He was getting angry both at Torrance and at himself for believing him. He wasn't able to do a thing with Airman Ash on cross-examination. Ash was insistent that Torrance hadn't been at Blake's any time that night; he remembered that because the night before Torrance had been raging about how his girlfriend had lied about seeing someone else, and he'd expected to hear more about it on the night of January 28th and 29th, but Torrance never showed up. Ash was a straightforward, credible witness.

It was four o'clock and already getting dark outside. Colonel Grundig asked Tom Donovan if he had a witness who wouldn't take too long, so that they could finish with him and recess by about four-thirty.

Donovan said he did, and called Staff Sergeant Emilio Hernandez of the Air Police records section. They had to wait almost ten minutes for him to arrive. Hernandez hadn't planned to testify that afternoon.

"Sergeant Hernandez," Donovan asked after his witness shook the snow off his coat and boots, took the stand

and was sworn in. "Would you tell us what sort of records are maintained of visitors to the base."

"Sure," Hernandez answered. "We keep a permanent record of all vehicles and all people who come onto the base. The records are cross-indexed by license plate numbers, make and color of car, drivers and passengers. This is a SAC bomber base, sir, with heavy weapons on board." There was a hint of condescension in his voice, as though Donovan had forgotten what sort of place Wurtsmith was. "It's a security matter."

Donovan nodded, without commenting. He knew exactly what he was dealing with. "Sergeant, do you have with you the Air Police records of visitors to the base on the night of last January 8th?" he asked.

"Yes, sir. In fact, I have the records covering that entire week here." Sergeant Hernandez held up an inch thick three-ring binder.

Tony felt an uneasy sensation in the pit of his stomach. He knew where this was going.

"Sergeant, I'd like you to examine those records right now, and tell the Court whether you have any record of a Lucy Jenks coming on base the night of January 8th, and leaving the next morning?" The room was quiet as Donovan asked his question; while the Sergeant was looking Donovan augmented his question by adding the color and make of the car. .

Sergeant Hernandez looked through his records for about a minute before responding.

"No sir, we have no record of anyone by that name or

a vehicle of that description coming on base that night, or leaving the next morning, sir."

"Check the day before, sergeant," Donovan said, "as well as the day after."

Sergeant Hernandez flipped the pages forward and back, then looked up at Donovan, "No one by that name or in a vehicle like that entered or left the base any time that week, sir," he said.

Tom Donovan nodded as he walked away from the witness. Turning he asked. "Check it again, Sergeant," he said from the far side of the courtroom. "But this time check for a Chevrolet pick-up with Michigan license plate number BB-126. I believe that's Miss Jenk's car."

Hernandez thumbed through his records again. "No sir, no vehicle with that license plate came on base at any time that week," he said firmly.

Son-of-a-bitch! Tony said to himself. *I believed her! They both lied to me; Torrance and his damn girlfriend!* He slumped back in his chair, his mind unable to focus on anything.

"I didn't know they maintained those kinds of records this long," he whispered aloud, staring straight ahead.

"Neither did I," Wally whispered back, "If that's any consolation, but now we do."

At Donovan's request, the relevant Air Police records for the week were formally identified as part of the court's exhibit box to be introduced with the rest of the prosecution's exhibits at the close of his case.

"No questions!" Tony snapped when Donovan had

finished with Sergeant Hernandez. Colonel Grundig gaveled the proceedings recessed, and everyone rose to leave.

Tony abruptly walked away from the defense table and stepped out into the hall. He didn't want to be anywhere near Torrance. *The lying bastard is guilty as hell! There isn't any doubt about it now.* Out in the hall, Tony turned away from the exiting crowd, trying hard to control his anger.

"You've got a tough case to defend, Captain," a friendly voice said behind him. It was Major Davis. "A damn tough case," Davis repeated, lighting up a Lucky.

"That's for sure!" Tony fumed. "The son-of-a-bitch hasn't been straight with me once! He sits there and says he's not guilty, and now all this shit comes out! Who would believe him now?"

"I sure don't," Davis responded and took a heavy draw, then slowly exhaled. "And I can't imagine that you do either, do you?"

"Hell no, not anymore!" Tony clenched his teeth and shook his head. He'd never felt this angry before. More than just angry, he felt *betrayed*. He had believed George Torrance.

"No one's going to fault you if you don't win this case," Davis continued, patting Tony on the shoulder. "You've done everything you could. It's perfectly obvious that Torrance is guilty. Wouldn't you say?"

"I can't argue with you on that." Tony replied, half to himself as he stared out the window at the endless new snow, trying to sort out all the damaging evidence that had been thrown at him that day.

Tony stepped over to the drinking fountain and took a gulp of cold water. It helped him calm down. He turned back to Davis, "Forgive me Major, for getting so angry."

"Don't worry," Davis said smiling, "I understand."

Chapter 10

—*mm*—

Tony pulled off his tie when he got home, gave Karen a perfunctory kiss, and poured himself some Cutty. He plopped down on their couch and stared at his glass.

"Doesn't look like the trial's going well," she said as she walked over to him.

"It's going terribly; just terribly."

"What do you mean?" Karen sat down close to Tony on the couch.

"That lying son-of-a-bitch killed both those women," Tony said, shaking his head. "He really conned me." He took a healthy swig of his scotch. "Everything he told me was a lie," he said, turning to Karen. "*Everything*." And it all came out today. How the hell am I supposed to defend someone who I know is guilty, and he lies to me about everything?" Tony took another drink, leaned back and shut his eyes. He felt like every bit of energy had been drained out of him.

Karen slid over and began rubbing the back of Tony's neck. It felt good.

"Dinner's almost ready," she said quietly after a few minutes. "Feel like eating?"

"Not really; not now," Tony said, his eyes still shut.

"I understand, I really do," she answered, still rubbing his neck. "Well, if you do get hungry, I made some Lasagna and Bolognese sauce, your favorite, I recall. I might have a bite or two now, and put the rest in the oven to keep it warm, if you do get hungry." She leaned over, kissed him on the cheek, rose and walked into the kitchen.

"Okay, thanks."

Karen served herself and sat down quietly. Tony could tell from its aroma that she had cooked it with mushrooms. He loved mushrooms. As far as Tony was concerned, everything should be cooked with mushrooms. Maybe he was a little hungry after all. He rose, slowly walked into the kitchen and gave Karen a little smile. "I changed my mind," he said quietly as he pulled up a chair and sat down across from her. As they ate he told her about some of the high and low points of the day's trial; almost all bad. After a while, Karen looked up at her husband. "Tony, why don't you just withdraw from the case?" she said quietly. "It's tearing you apart. They can't make you defend Torrance, can they?"

"I don't know," Tony answered quietly. "There are ethical rules about that sort of thing. I can't just quit in the middle of a trial. After all, he *is* entitled to the right to counsel, and I'm his appointed counsel, like it or not. He still insists he's not guilty, so that's the approach I'm ethically obligated to follow, even if I know in my gut he's a lying son-of-a-bitch." Tony put his fork down, took off his glasses and rubbed his eyes. "I just don't know what to do; in debate or moot court, even if I had a weak case, I could always spot the weakness in my opponent's case, tear into it and make it appear to be the center point of the issue. That's why I almost always won. But I don't see a weak spot here. None. And I don't even have a client who's cooperating or being honest with me," he said. "What in the hell am I doing in the middle of a murder trial anyway? A few months ago I was doing research in the library for an article for Professor Malcom Sharp." He added after a moment. "This is insane."

Karen started to speak, but Tony went on. "And what the hell are we even doing in the Air Force? I'm no soldier, I'm a fucking lawyer. One day I'm having a couple of beers with friends at Jimmy's on 55th Street, and the next thing I know I'm working on a case, which if I lose, and I probably will, the defendant is put to death! By a firing squad. Dead! This whole thing is insane."

"It could be worse, Tony," Karen said softly. "I was talking to Marla Watson today. She's taking Charlie's body back to Connecticut tomorrow. After that, she doesn't have a clue what she's going to do."

"You're right," Tony nodded. "It could be worse."

The shrill ring of the telephone startled them both. Tony put his glasses back on, pushed his chair back and walked into the living room to answer it.

"Hello," he said wearily.

"Tony, its Wally. I'm at the stockade. I've been

talking to Torrance. I think you'd better get down here right away."

"Wally, I don't know about you, but I'm beat," Tony answered. "And I sure as hell don't feel like going out right now and busting my butt for George Torrance. I'm not sure I want to even represent him anymore."

"I know what you mean; but believe me, this is important."

McDonald sounded concerned. Tony decided that he owed it to him, if not Torrance, to get on over to the Air Police compound.

"I don't know how long this is going to take," he told Karen with resignation.

McDonald was waiting for Tony when he walked into the front hallway of the Air Police compound. His darting eyes exuded excitement.

"Tony, thanks for coming over. I've got Torrance in one of the back rooms. You've got to hear what he has to say."

"I don't care what the son-of-a-bitch has to say to us, Wally. It's just going to be some more lies, like everything else he's ever told us."

"I'm not sure they *have* been all lies," Wally said as he pushed open the inside door and led Tony into the waiting room. It was empty except for a staff sergeant behind the counter and an airman in back typing. To the right was a door leading to the prisoner detention area.

"Sign in here, captain." The sergeant pushed a registration book across the counter.

At the sergeant's direction, the young airman unlocked the door at the end of the counter and led the two officers down the concrete-block corridor to the rear. They were taken to the same small room where they had first met Torrance. When they walked in he was sitting on a metal chair, leaning up against the far wall and watching the door. Three steel chairs surrounded a small gray table; probably, Tony thought, the same steel furnishings that had been there previously.

"Tell Captain Jeffries what you told me," Wally said to Torrance once they were alone. Torrance gave Tony a hard look, scowled and rocked his chair forward. The two officers took seats at the table.

"There was a heap of bullshit goin' on t'day, Cap'n."

"What do you mean?" Tony said, tiredly.

"Ash, for one. He knows damn good that I's at the bar. He's just fuckin' lyin'."

Tony knew it was going to be like this. Torrance was giving them the same story, with maybe some new emphasis. Tony's tolerance level was very low. He wasn't going to waste his time with this.

"Come on, George," he snapped. "I've had it with your bullshit. Why would Ash lie? What difference would it make to him if you were at Blake's that night or not? And what about the Air Police records? Lucy never drove on base that first night. Are you saying they faked the records?"

"No, man. They never knew'd she was here. She din't use *their* gate. Comin' or goin'."

"What do you mean '*their* gate'?" Tony asked. "There's only one gate into the base, George. And it's covered by AP's around the clock."

George shook his head and leaned his chair against the cold concrete-block wall. He kept his eyes on Tony as he pulled a pack of Luckies out of his jump suit pocket and lit one up. He took a deep drag and exhaled a cloud of smoke, flipping his pack onto the table as he sat forward.

"There's another gate. You guys new 'round here, so you probably don't even know 'bout it."

"Another gate? Where?"

"On the south side. Not supposed to use it. But what the hell."

"Are you talking about an unmanned gate?"

"Yeah. Maintenance gate."

"Isn't it locked?" Tony asked.

"Sure, but that's no problem, man," Torrance grinned.

Wally turned to Tony. "What he's saying, Tony, is that he let Lucy in through *that* gate, and out again the same way the next morning. That way they wouldn't be hassled for her spending the night on base. *That's* why the Air Police don't have a record of her car being here."

"Tha's right," Torrance said, rocking his chair back up against the wall. "You never done axe me before what gate she come in."

Tony didn't believe him for a second. This was pure bullshit, and he knew it. He was surprised that Wally gave it any credence at all. Tony decided to show McDonald that Torrance was conning them again.

"All right, George," Tony said. "In that case, you should be able to take us to that gate right now. And show us how you can open the lock by yourself. Do you have any problem with that, George?"

"You can't git me outta here, Cap'n," Torrance said with a smile.

"Let me worry about that," Tony answered. "But if I can get you out, can you show us that back gate and how to open it?"

"No problem, man." Torrance's brass amazed him.

Tony managed to arrange for them to take Torrance out of the stockade for an hour. The requirements were that an armed air policeman accompany them and that they not leave the Base. Staff Sergeant Mike Dahlke drew the assignment; he had just come in from patrol duty. It was a bitter cold night, and he wasn't happy about having to go back out.

They drove around to the back side of the base in Wally's Plymouth with Tony next to him. Torrance sat in back, gaving Wally directions; Dahlke was next to him with his automatic rifle in his lap, aimed at Torrance.

Torrance directed Wally to bring the car to a halt on the perimeter road south of the runway. "This be it," he said.

Multiple tire tracks ran off to the south, forming a lane through the snow. The four men got out and began following it; all were carrying flashlights, including Torrance with his cuffed hands. He was in front, with his uniform cap perched atop his afro, followed by Dahlke with his gun. The lawyers followed. After about thirty yards they came to the base's outer chain-link fence. It was eight feet high, topped with barbed wire, and had a locked maintenance gate. The tracks went through, continuing on the far side into the darkness.

"This be the place where I done let her in," Torrance said to Tony. "And out again the next day."

"So, let's see you open the lock, George." Tony replied with contempt.

Torrance walked over to the gate, turned the padlock with his cuffed hands, so that it hung up against the metal gate post, raised his boot, and gave the lock a hard kick. It popped open.

"Damn!" Tony said aloud.

Torrance hung the open padlock on the gate. The gate had been used so often that most of the snow was already clear of its opening arc. Torrance had easily pushed it open. He turned to the other three gesturing as though waving a truck through. He had proven his point. He turned back and faced the open gate and the darkness beyond.

A metallic click broke the momentary silence. Sergeant Dahlke had flicked the safety off his rifle and had it aimed directly at Torrance's back.

"Be cool, man," Torrance said as he slowly turned, raising his arms. He smiled at Dahlke. The sergeant kept his gun leveled at Torrance. He wasn't smiling.

"Come on, Wally, let's get this gate secured," Tony said. McDonald helped him close and lock the gate. Tony yanked the lock, it was secure.

"I think we'd better get back to the stockade," Sergeant Dahlke said crisply, his gun still at the ready. No one objected. As the others started back to the car, Tony stopped and turned to take a close look at the lock and make some notes.

They drove back to the Air Police compound and dropped off Sergeant Dahlke and his prisoner. "We'll see you in the morning, George," Tony told Torrance.

He and McDonald sat in the car and talked for a long time. "That alibi for January 8th seems a lot more viable now," Wally said.

"I'm not convinced," Tony replied. "All that Torrance proved tonight was that there's a back gate and that he knows how to open it. There's no evidence that Lucy Jenks came in that way on the 8th. I think Torrance came up with this story after the Air Police shot his first story down." Tony paused, adding, "As far as I'm concerned, George Torrance is still a lying bastard."

"But you've got to admit it gives his alibi for January 8th a little more plausibility," McDonald persisted.

"Sure; a little," Tony answered. "But what's the difference. His alibi for the second night, early on the 29th, was destroyed by Ash. You said yourself that you couldn't find anyone at Blake's who would confirm that Torrance was there that night. And those are his *friends*. That blows his story out of the water. He's the goddamn killer, Wally, face it."

"Tony, I want to check Blake's one more time. Right now. Will you go there with me?"

"Are you *serious*?" Tony looked at his watch; it was almost nine o'clock.

"Yes I am. We still might come up with something. Besides, I'll buy you a beer to make it worth your while."

"On that condition, all right. But I still think it's a complete waste of time."

McDonald drove out the main gate of the base past the area where the anti-war protestors stood and chanted during the day, turned south, then turned right on River Road. After about five minutes he pulled to a stop in front of a small one-story wooden building with a half dozen cars parked in front in the snow. The single light bulb hanging over the front door illuminated an old Budweiser sign and the weathered words "Blake's Tavern."

It was difficult for them to adjust to the dim light when they pushed open the door and entered. Smoke rising from a dozen cigarettes muddied the air. Small groups of men, all black, at several tables stopped talking and watched the two white officers make their way to the bar. Tony felt uncomfortable, very uncomfortable.

Eugene Ash, in civvies, was the bartender. He looked at them, walked over, and asked them what they wanted. "Two Buds," Wally said, "and some more information about George Torrance." Ash spat into a spittoon behind the bar, opened two bottles and said that he didn't have anything more to say. He walked down to the far end of the bar to talk to another customer.

Wally took a swallow of his Bud and glanced around the room. "What are you looking for?" Tony asked.

"I'm trying to figure out who's most likely to talk to us."

"Good luck." Tony shook his head knowing it was useless and took a swig of his beer. As he put the bottle down he noticed a flashing light out of the corner of his eye.

A moment later the wooden door swung open and a shadowy figure stepped into the bar. The pulsating lights of a squad car parked behind him made it hard to discern his features. As he approached the bar Tony could see that he was wearing a brown uniform and a flat Sheriff's hat.

"Can I help you, Sheriff?" The bartender asked as he walked over.

"Let me see your liquor license, Ash."

"It's right there on the wall, Sheriff," the bartender gestured to a framed certificate behind the bar.

"Give it to me. I can't read that from here."

The Sheriff took the framed license that Ash handed him, peered at it in the dim light, and after what seemed like an eternity, pushed it back across the bar.

"Seems to be in order," he said, turning and looking down the bar at Tony and Wally. They were about ten feet away, watching him, as was everyone else. The rhythmic red flashes through the half-open door reflected off the brass on the officers' shoulders. The Sheriff stepped over to them.

"I'm Ben Chapman," he said, looking from one to the other. "You might recall that we met a while ago when you guys were investigating the first murder case." Tony nodded without comment. "You boys are a little out of your element here, aren't you?" He was a big, but wiry man, and even in the shadows of the bar Tony could tell he was in good shape. He also couldn't help but noticing that Chapman's right hand never left the handle of his side arm.

"Not necessarily, Sheriff," Tony answered. "We just stopped by for a beer."

"Officers from the base don't just stop by *this* place for a beer, Captain. Especially white officers. You boys could get in serious trouble by coming here, do you know that?"

"I think we can take care of ourselves, officer," Tony replied. This two-bit local cop was beginning to irritate him.

"Just concerned about your welfare, Captain. Wouldn't want you to miss the rest of your trial." He touched the brim of his hat in a hint of a salute, smiled, and walked out.

When the door shut, Wally turned to Tony with wide open eyes. "Tony, that guy knew who we were and that we were here, at Blake's."

"Sure seems that way." Tony took a deep drink of his

Bud. He had the distinct sense that they had just been leaned on.

"Well, let's do what we came here to do," McDonald said. He picked up his beer and walked over to a nearby table where three men, all airmen in wrinkled uniforms, were quietly talking. Tony followed him.

"Mind if we join you?" McDonald asked.

One of the men shrugged and gestured to the two empty seats. They were all low-ranking airman, probably in their early twenties, Tony noted. "We're George Torrance's lawyers," Wally said. The men acknowledged that they knew Torrance.

McDonald told them that it was important that they find someone who could verify that Torrance was at Blake's the night the second killing occurred. Ash had testified that Torrance hadn't been there, but they thought he was wrong. George's life probably depended on what they could come up with, McDonald said.

Tony let Wally do all the talking. He still wasn't sure it was a good idea for them to be there, and kept his eyes scanning the room as Wally went on.

The three airmen didn't respond, even after Wally rephrased and repeated his questions. They just stared ahead at their drinks. Finally, one of them looked up and muttered quietly, "Don't git us involved, 'tenant!"

"Involved?" McDonald answered. "We're just trying to find out if he was here."

"Go talk to Buddha," one of the airman pointed over his shoulder. "We got nothin' to say."

The two officers turned and tried to focus their vision through the bar's dark smoky air. In the far corner table was an old man with short gray curly hair. Two younger men, sharing his table were conversing. The older man was leaning back with his eyes half shut, watching the white officers.

"Buddha," McDonald said quietly to Tony as they rose. "That's one of the names George gave me. I came here twice but wasn't able to find him."

"Well, so now you have," Tony replied skeptically.

They got up, nodded to the others, walked over to the corner table; again, with McDonald taking the lead. As they approached, the old man said something and the two younger men got up and left. "Are you Buddha?" McDonald asked.

"That's what they call me." He nodded at the two empty chairs. "Sit down."

"We're George Torrance's law…"

"I *know* who you are and why you're here," the older man cut him off in a deep gravelly voice.

Wally eased into the wooden chair across from Buddha. "We need some help."

"No, you mean *George* needs some help, don't you?"

"Yes, I'm sorry," McDonald corrected himself.

Buddha leaned back, looking at them. He was a large man. Not that tall, Tony supposed, but solid; he probably weighed about two hundred and twenty pounds. His face was full and he was wearing an old uniform shirt with the insignias torn off. He looked too old to be in the Air

Force, but had to have some connection with the base or he wouldn't be there. As Buddha lifted his glass, Tony noticed that the middle finger of his left hand was missing.

"We'd like to know if someone saw George Torrance here at Blake's the early morning of January 29th, the night of the second murder," Wally continued.

"Why do you want to know *that*?"

"We're trying to confirm that George Torrance was here that night, as he claims. It would go a long way in establishing his defense if we had some testimony that he was here." Wally answered.

"Whether George was here or not?" the old man said quizzically. He smiled and chuckled to himself. "Hell, all you want is to avoid being embarrassed too badly by that hot shot trial lawyer they brung in to bury George."

"So you know Captain Donovan?" Tony asked, leaning forward.

"Hell, everyone knows who Donovan is, 'cept you two I guess. He's the best goddamn trial lawyer in the Air Force. You boys are in the process of being fucked. Hasn't that dawned on you?"

"What are you talking about?"

"Any man here could make your case if they wanted to."

The old man waved his big right arm around the rest of the room. "The fact is that every man here saw George that night."

"What?"

"That's right. George was here; just like he said. All

night, after 'bout 'leven thirty."

Tony was dumbstruck. *The case had just been turned upside down.*

"But nobody would confirm that," Wally stammered. "I was here before, and talked to some of these men, and nobody could remember anything."

"That's 'cause nobody's goin' to testify in court," the old man answered leaning forward and looking Wally in his eyes. He paused for a moment, keeping his eyes on Wally's. "Don't you get it? The man was guilty before he was arrested. Nobody even asked him what his story was. He's goin' down. Everybody knows that. Any colored folk who help him are goin' down, too."

Ash had walked up to the table and interrupted, wiping a heavy beer mug with a bar towel. "Any problem, Buddha?"

"No problem." The old man waved him away. Ash glanced at the two officers, before stepping back and heading for the bar.

"Oh, and we'll buy Buddha a drink," Wally said aloud. Ash turned slightly, nodded, then made his way back to the bar. Buddha took a sip from his half-full glass of whiskey. "What you boys don't understand," he said, "*any* negro will do, as long as the story fits. And the story fit George."

Tony's mind was swimming. He had a hundred questions to ask, but couldn't verbalize a single one.

"How can you just let this happen?" Wally whispered. "This is terrible."

"Easy 'nough for you to say, Lieutenant. You've gone

to college and law school, and you're goin' to get out of the service as fast as you can, ain't you?"

"Well, I probably am. So what?"

"So, you're gonna be a rich lawyer. Live in a big house. Kids'll go to college. You can walk away from the service. Hell, you *plan* to walk away. Guys like us, though…" he gestured again around the room, "we work for the service all our lives. What else we gonna do? Only pension we'll ever get. Hell, I cross The Man, and I'm back in the alleys of Birmingham in no time. Never work again. Or worse."

Buddha sipped his drink again, as he looked at the two young men. "And that's why nobody's gonna testify that George was here. I say, nobody!"

They tried to reason with him, even argue with him, but it was useless. Finally, they rose to leave. As they did, McDonald left a five on the table for the drinks, asked him to at least consider testifying, but Buddha just shook his head and looked down.

Snow was falling as they walked out into the parking lot. Tony turned to McDonald. For a moment he couldn't speak. "Wally," he said at last, "Torrance really *is* innocent." His mind seemed paralyzed, and he shook his head to clear it. "We've *got* to do something. More than what we've done so far."

McDonald nodded, but was staring at something behind Tony. Finally, he pointed in disbelief.

"Yeah, but first we'll have to figure out how to get back to base," he said. The two left tires of his Plymouth were flat. They had been slashed.

Chapter 11

—*ww*—

It continued snowing heavily all that night. By the time it stopped on Friday morning, twenty-eight inches of fresh snow had fallen across northern Michigan. That delighted the skiers at Boyne Mountain, but it made driving in the area impossible. On top of the deep base of snow that was already there, the new drifts completely covered any vehicles that had been left outside. Some would not be seen again until spring.

On base, the main roads were kept open, but no effort was made to plow driveways or parking lots. Narrow walkways were shoveled from building entrances to the few cleared lanes. The snow on both sides of those paths was often piled six or seven feet high. Everyone put on their heavy winter gear and walked when they had to go out. A few people traveled by cross-country skis.

The runways, of course, had to be kept clear at all times. The bombers on alert still had to be able to be off the ground within five minutes, regardless of the weather.

When the snow began falling on Thursday night, a fleet of giant plows began sweeping up and down the main runway at thirty miles an hour. Traveling together, they threw a continuous wall of churning snow a hundred feet into the air. They never stopped for two days, except to refuel and change crews every four hours.

Tony hadn't gotten back to the apartment until after midnight the night before. He and Wally had trekked about half-way back through the snow before a passing motorist took pity on them and drove them to the base's main gate. Karen was still up and worried. A hot bath and a shot of whiskey helped warm him, but Tony still couldn't fall asleep. He was awake all night thinking about the trial.

The prosecution's case was like a locomotive, building up steam and barreling down the tracks. So far, Tony hadn't done anything to slow it down. But he wasn't sure he had tried very hard. He hadn't done anything creative, or even very aggressive. Maybe that was because he had increasingly felt in his gut that George Torrance really had raped and killed those two women. Worse than that; *yesterday* he was sure of it. But now he was just as sure Torrance was innocent, he *knew* it, and felt a desperate need to do something to save him.

Ruth Olmsted, the court reporter, arrived a little after ten; she had to wait for the plow to clear her road before she could drive in from Oscoda. The courtroom was about three-quarters full when she got there, although they were still missing several court members. The snow kept away most of the townspeople who had been following the trial. McDonald wasn't there; he had gone to salvage his car outside Blake's. Tony would have to begin without him. While waiting, Donovan advised the court that when the trial resumed, his next witness would be Bill Carlson, one of the eye-witnesses.

After another hour's wait, an airman in a parka walked up to Colonel Grundig from the side of the courtroom saluted and handed him a folded piece of paper. He stood waiting, his snow-covered boots dripping on the tile floor, while Grundig read the message. The colonel nodded, said something to the young man, who saluted again clumsily in his heavy coat and left through the side door.

It was almost noon and Grundig rose to make an announcement. The room quickly quieted. "The trial will not resume today," he said. Two of the court members, Major Smithfield and Sergeant Longtree, have emergency duties related to the blizzard that has struck the base, and since it is essential that it be operable at all times, the court will remain in recess until nine o'clock next Monday morning.

Tony's immediate reaction was relief. They now had two and a half days to pull their case together.

Law books, yellow pads, and various documents covered the living room floor in the Jeffries' apartment that Saturday night. Tony and Wally were engrossed in every aspect of the case trying to finalize a viable defense for

Torrance, while Karen and Patty combined the contents of their refrigerators, used some ingenuity, and were preparing dinner.

The aroma of cannelloni cooking in the oven reminded everyone that they'd been working all day and were getting hungry. It was seven o'clock when they sat down for dinner.

Inevitably, the phone rang; Tony reached over and grabbed it. "Yes," he barked.

"Hello, Tony. This is Bob Cunningham. I'm calling from Milwaukee. How do you like being a trial lawyer?"

It took Tony a moment to refocus. "Bob, how are you? Geez, it's good to hear your voice." Turning to the others as he covered the phone with his hand, he said, "It's Bob Cunningham. This may be important to the case."

"I just heard that you're defending the murder case," Cunningham continued. "That's heavy stuff. How's it going?" His voice sounded far away.

"Rough, Bob. They're trying to nail him. And the damn thing is that he's not guilty. I'm convinced of that."

"That's why I'm not there," Cunningham said. "I finally figured out why they sent me here with such a big trial approaching."

The thought struck Tony like a thunderbolt. Of course; it suddenly became crystal clear. It matched what Buddha had said to them at Blake's. The whole trial was contrived to convict Torrance! Including Tony's role! He stared out the window into the swirling snow and slowly lowered the phone.

"Are you there, Tony?" Cunningham's voice crackled over the line.

"Yes, I'm here," Tony said quietly as he picked the phone back up. He hesitated a moment, then pleaded, "Look Bob, I could use your advice. I may be in over my head."

"Easy, Tony." Cunningham said. "Let's talk about it."

Tony gestured for the others to go on with dinner as he took the phone with its long cord into the living room. "Go ahead, Bob," he answered, grabbing a yellow pad and a pen as he sat down.

Bob had Tony run through the witnesses and evidence that had been presented by the prosecution so far. He asked questions about the appearance and demeanor of the witnesses. Then they talked about the cross-examination of the remaining prosecution witnesses, and Tony's planned presentation of the defense case.

Cunningham told Tony what he knew about the men on the court. Grundig and Smithfield, in particular, were going to support the prosecution no matter what the evidence showed. He was confident that's why they had been appointed. The two sergeants weren't going to be any help either. If the defense had any chance at all, it had to be through Colonel Bolte. He was hard-nosed, but fair. Cunningham didn't know anything about the two younger officers, Fanzone and Kopecky.

They talked for over an hour, Tony scribbling notes continuously. At one point, Tony had to take a quick break and grab another yellow pad. When Tony finally hung up, he had a much clearer picture of what he had to do.

He was also angry. If Colonel Breckenridge and those bastards thought that Tony Jeffries was a patsy because he was young, they were wrong. Several good trial tactics had coalesced in his mind while he was discussing the case with Cunningham. If they wanted a trial, then by God, he'd show them a trial! He *wasn't* going to lose this case!

Tony walked over to the dining room table and joined the others; their conversation stopped and they all looked at Tony quizzically. "Karen and Patty" he said after a moment, "when we're done I'd appreciate it if you can find all the magazines and newspapers we have, look through them, and cut out any pictures or ads of pickups with campers."

—*mm*—

When the court martial resumed on Monday morning, Tom Donovan called his first witness, William Carlson.

"Just a minute," Tony said, immediately rising from the defense table before Carlson could be brought into the room. "This next witness is being called to identify the defendant as driving away from the scene of the first murder. We all know that. But there's a serious question as to whether this witness can actually identify the defendant.

We'd like to test that in court today."

"That's no problem, counselor," Donovan replied. "I'll just ask the witness at the appropriate time if the man he saw that night is in the courtroom today. If he identifies the defendant, that will resolve the issue."

"No, it won't. He knows that the defendant will be sitting right here," Tony retorted, pointing at Torrance's chair. "He's probably been told that already. We understand that there hasn't been a line-up identification in this case. The only fair test now will be to have the defendant switch seats with someone else in the room. Another black airman. Then see who Mr. Carlson identifies."

"Really, Captain Jeffries," Donovan laughed. "That's absurd. This is a trial, not some sort of a party game."

"I agree," Colonel Grundig added. "I think it's highly irregular and completely unnecessary. Bring your witness in, Captain Donovan."

"Wait a minute," the officer seated at Grundig's left spoke up. It was Lieutenant Colonel Michael Bolte. "If I might comment, sir, this is a murder case. The prosecution's asking for the death penalty. I think Captain Jeffries' request is reasonable. If we end up convicting the defendant, I don't want anyone to be able to say that we didn't give him a decent shake particularly if we impose the death penalty."

Colonel Grundig looked uncertainly up and down the court.

"With your leave, sir, that sounds fair to me," Captain Angelo Fanzone added from the right side of the table.

"Well, I strongly object, gentlemen!" Donovan said. He looked to Colonel Goldsmith for a ruling on his objection.

Mel Goldsmith was caught off guard. Aware of the consequences, and not knowing how to rule, he quickly passed the buck. "There isn't any rule of law involved," he said defensively. "I think it's discretionary with the court."

"Why *not* let Captain Jeffries do it." Angelo Fanzone said. "I'm curious now to see what this next witness will do."

"All right," Grundig said reluctantly, "Go ahead, Captain Jeffries."

Tony was excited, he had finally, successfully seized control. This was a desperate move, but he had to do something to shake up the prosecution's case. The idea had struck Tony early Sunday morning. He got dressed, had a quick cup of coffee and went to the Base's Personnel Office, looking for someone who could let him in. Luckily he found an airman there catching up on his work. Tony quickly scanned the photos of all enlisted personnel on base and picked out a black airman who somewhat resembled Torrance but who didn't have a mustache, which Torrance did; Tony located the airman and instructed him to be at the Court Martial when it reconvened Monday morning in The Headquarters Building. Receiving those instructions from a captain, the airman felt he had no alternative but to comply. He was there. Torrance, of course, was there but without his mustache, which he had shaved off at Tony's instruction.

Colonel Bolte, sitting next to Colonel Grundig on the court, admonished Donovan not to say a word to the witness about the switch. Donovan agreed, and called in Bill Carlson.

"I know we discussed this, but do you know what you're doing?" Wally whispered to Tony. He had slipped in next to Tony during the discussions.

"It might work. Besides, we've got nothing to lose," Tony whispered in response.

"Sure we have something to lose. What if Carlson says the guy sitting in the back of the courtroom is the one he saw driving away that night? That would ice it for Donovan. And good morning to you too; I was up all night dealing with the damn car."

"I hadn't thought about Carlson actually picking out Torrance," Tony said quietly. "Anyway, it's too late now."

Bill Carlson was a thin young man of about five-foot ten, with medium-length blond hair and acne scars on his cheeks and forehead. He was wearing a green wool sweater and khaki pants. Donovan asked him a series of questions about his background designed to put him at ease, and to establish some rapport between him and the court. Carlson testified that he was a senior at Iosco County Consolidate High School and hoped to go to Michigan State next fall.

"Will you tell us where you were, Bill, the night of January 8th," Donovan asked easily. "About nine or ten o'clock."

"Sure. My girlfriend, Brenda, and I had been driving around in the State Forest, and we stopped on the county road just outside the Base; about halfway down the runway. That's the road that comes straight south to the Base, turns right and follows the fence." Carlson gesticulated as he spoke. By their nods, everyone on the court indicated that they knew what road he was talking about.

"By the way, Bill, just for the record, what's your girlfriend's full name?" Donovan inquired.

"Brenda Wendt," the young man answered. "Brenda Maria Wendt."

"Thank you. Now, were you parked on the road that parallels the fence?"

"No, sir. We were parked on the section of the road that comes through the forest up to the Base, before it turns."

"So that you and Brenda were facing the Base as you sat there, is that right?"

"Right. At the edge of the woods. It's fun to watch the planes take off and land from there. Sometimes lots of planes take off all at one time; that's really exciting."

"Did you see anything unusual that night, Bill?" Donovan asked. Several men on the court leaned forward.

"Yes. About nine-thirty we saw this pickup truck tearing along the road on the inside of the fence in our direction. We noticed it because it was going so fast; really bouncing along. It passed right in front of us, and kept on going to the right."

"What kind of a pickup truck was it, Bill? Could you

tell?" Donovan was talking now like an old friendly camp counselor.

"Yes, sir," the young man answered. "It was a Ford pickup with a camper."

"It was bright enough to see that?" Donovan asked.

"Oh yes, sir. There was a full moon. It was very bright that night."

"Was it bright enough to see the driver of the truck, Bill?"

"Yes, it was. We saw that driver. He went right in front of us. He was colored."

"Is the man you saw in this courtroom today, Bill?" Donovan asked, raising his voice. "Be real sure before you answer."

"Yes, he's right there." Carlson said, pointing to the black airman sitting at the defense table next to Tony. Donovan grimaced and turned away.

Tony jumped to his feet. "Would the defendant, Airman Torrance, please rise." George Torrance stood in the last row of spectators. He was grinning. The reporters in the front row were scribbling notes. Others in the audience began whispering to each other.

"I want the record to reflect the fact that Mr. Carlson has identified the wrong man," Tony said. "The witness has identified Airman Second Class Donald Adams, who arrived at Wurtsmith two weeks ago. He was at Lackland Air Force Base in Texas on January 8th. Isn't that right, Airman Adams?"

"Yes, sir. Yes it is." Adams said as he rose to his feet,

a nervous smile on his face.

"Wait a minute," Carlson stammered. "I'm sorry. *That's* the man we saw." He pointed weakly at George Torrance; standing in the back of the room.

"Too late, son," Colonel Bolte said, shaking his head.

"I move for the immediate dismissal of the charges against Airman Torrance," Tony said. "If the key prosecution witness can't identify him, what are we all doing here?"

"This is a very small part of the prosecution's case," Donovan calmly answered. "Mr. Carlson's identification of the defendant was frosting on the cake. We're fully prepared to prove Airman Torrance's guilt without Mr. Carlson's identification."

"Based on that representation, the defendant's motion to dismiss is denied," Colonel Goldsmith ruled.

Colonel Grundig excused Airman Adams who almost ran from the room. Torrance came forward and took his place at the defense table. Tony had made his point.

"Nice going!" Wally whispered.

Donovan had no further questions for Carlson and tendered him to Jeffries for cross.

Tony stood and came around to the front of the defense table. "Mr. Carlson," he asked, "You said the man you saw was driving a Ford pickup. Would you describe for us the differences between Ford and Chevy pickup trucks, when viewed from the side?"

"Well...." The witness shifted uncomfortably in his chair.

"Let's start first with the chrome," Tony continued. "How would you compare the chrome on the side of a Ford pickup with the chrome on the side of a Chevy pickup?"

Bill Carlson hesitated again before answering. Tony picked a manila folder off the defense table, opened it and pulled out a sheet of paper. He glanced down at it, and looked up at Carlson.

"Does a Chevy pickup have *any* chrome on the side, Mr. Carlson?"

"I'm not sure," Carlson stammered.

"Pardon me?"

"I can't answer that. I don't know." Another longer pause caught everyone's attention. "Actually, it was Brenda who recognized that truck as a Ford. She really knows pickup trucks. Better than I do."

"I see," Tony said as he laid the folder and the sheet of paper down on the table behind him. Wally McDonald looked over at the paper. It was blank.

"So *you* can't swear, testifying under oath, what make of truck it was?" Jeffries asked.

"That's right. I can't, but Brenda can."

"Gentlemen," Tony said, turning to the court, "I move to strike Mr. Carlson's testimony that the truck he saw was a Ford. It's clear he had no basis for that testimony. Another witness, not Mr. Carlson, evidently made that identification."

Colonel Grundig looked at Goldsmith for a ruling. Goldsmith looked uncomfortable, hesitated, and reluctantly knew that he had no choice. The motion to strike was in order and would be granted. Carlson's testimony about the make of the truck would be stricken.

"Beautiful!" McDonald said as Tony sat down.

"It's the first thing we've done for Torrance in this whole damn trial," Tony replied quietly. "But I hope it's not too little and too late."

mm

That night a handful of hardy officers made their way through the drifts to the bar at the Officers' Club. For those men who had served at Anchorage or Thule, this weather was nothing. Certainly not enough to keep a good man from the comfort of his neighborhood saloon.

Two of the officers from the Torrance court martial were there, talking at the end of the bar; Major Clark Smithfield and Lieutenant John Kopecky. Smithfield, the Wing's chief munitions officer, had spent the past weekend insuring the safety and reliability of the Wing's nuclear weapons, particularly those loaded on the B-52's. With the resumption of the trial earlier that day, he was exhausted and needed a drink. Kopecky was bored to death at the Bachelor Officers' Quarters. There wasn't any action, his car was buried in snow so he couldn't get off base, and he wasn't on alert this week-end. He decided to go to the club to stupefy himself. He ran across Smithfield at the bar alone, watching the news of an anti-war demonstration in Berkeley.

"Damn fuckin' commies," Smithfield said, shaking his head and gesturing toward the TV.

"Aw, just a bunch of kids letting off steam," Kopecky answered after ordering a vodka martini. "Last year it was panty raids. No big deal. Look, when this war's over those guys will be trying to figure out what the hell they were bitching about."

"They don't have a clue, not a clue, what this is all about," Smithfield muttered. "And what about that Army Captain they murdered at Madison last month?" Smithfield continued. "Blew up the building his office was in. Killed him instantly. That's a hell of a lot more serious than a panty raid, if you ask me.

"Of course," Kopecky responded, "maybe they didn't mean to kill him, just screw up the Army Reserve program at Madison."

"Doesn't really matter," Smithfield answered. "Either way he's dead. Same as if he caught a sniper's shot to the head in Nam."

They sipped their drinks as the news shifted to other topics. It was natural before long that they'd get around to talking about something they had in common, the Court Martial.

They debated the impact of the various witness they had heard and items of evidence they had seen. Kopecky said he believed Torrance was probably guilty, but the testimony of that young man, Carlson, was giving him second thoughts.

Major Smithfield's response was curious. "I don't

have any reservations about Torrance's guilt. Torrance has killed and raped a woman before; in Macon, Georgia just before he joined the Air Force. He was never convicted; but the police didn't have any doubt about the fact that Torrance did it." He fired down his shot-glass of Johnny Walker Red and gestured to the bar tender for another, while Kopecky stared at him incredulously. "That showed the kind of person that Torrance is," Smithfield add, "He's a killer. Natural-born killer. Doesn't show up in his record though, since he was never formally charged."

"How the hell do you know that?"

Smithfield smiled and tapped his forehead; "I have my sources."

"You're sure about that."

"Absolutely," Smithfield said as the bar-keep refilled his glass. "Like I said, the man's a killer."

"Well, that's sure something to keep in mind."

Chapter 12

—⟶⟵—

The trial resumed Monday morning, February 26th, and the anti-war protestors who had vanished during the blizzard, reappeared at the main gate with their usual bull horns and signs. The roads had been cleared by now, and the court room was once again full to capacity. The number of civilians who wanted to watch the trial had increased dramatically because of the publicity it was receiving. None were allowed in unless they were members of the press, had been pre-approved, or could show that they worked on the base. Many spectators were lined up when the headquarters building opened at seven-thirty. By nine o'clock a thin blue haze of cigarette smoke hung over the room.

The prosecution called Brenda Wendt as its next witness. Brenda was a pretty redhead with blue eyes. She wore her hair shoulder length, was dressed in a pink sweater, light blue miniskirt and white knee-high boots. She gave Tom Donovan a smile as she took the stand.

Tony decided not to switch Torrance with someone else that day. That trick would only work once, and Tony was confident Brenda had heard all about it from Bill Carlson over the weekend.

After she was put under oath, Brenda repeated Carlson's account of seeing a Ford pickup truck with a camper driving on the back road away from the Officers' Club on the night of January 8th.

"Are you sure it was a *Ford* pickup, Brenda?" Donovan asked.

"Yes, I'm certain," she answered without hesitating.

"Why are you certain, Brenda?"

"Because our family has always owned Ford pickups," she said. "My dad gets a new one every other year. He's taken me with him to pick out the last three. Believe me, I *know* Ford pickups."

"Brenda, would you tell us the differences between a Ford pickup and a Chevy pickup, equipped with campers, when viewed from the side?" Donovan turned away from the court and winked at Tony. He was using Tony's own question to establish Brenda's credibility.

"Sure. For one thing, Fords have a chrome strip along the side, and Chevys don't. I think chrome strips look neat. Second, Ford bumpers wrap around a little," making a sweeping gesture with her right hand.

"Jesus Christ, Tony," Wally said under his breath. "She really *does* know Ford pickups."

"Finally," Brenda continued, "the windows are different. Ford windows are a little bit longer."

"And Brenda, you're confident that the truck you and Bill saw the night of January 8th was a *Ford*?" Donovan asked.

"Oh, yes," she said, nodding to the court.

Damn, she's good. Tony thought. *She's totally believable. She's got them eating out of her hands.*

"Did you see the driver of that truck, Brenda?" Donovan asked.

"Yes, I did."

"Is the man you saw in this courtroom today?"

Brenda looked at the defense table, hesitated, and looked to the back of the room. There were two black Airmen in the last row of spectators. She stared at them, then looked back at George Torrance.

"Well, Brenda, is the man you saw that night in this courtroom today?" Donovan asked again. Colonel Mike Bolte and several other men on the court leaned forward.

"I'm not..." She hesitated as her eyes frantically darted back and forth between the defense table and the rear of the room.

"Come now, Brenda, there's no need to be shy about it," Donovan said as he walked around the defense table and stood behind George Torrance.

"Can you point out the man you saw that night?" Donovan repeated, dropping his eyes as he finished the question.

"Yes, that's him." Brenda said quickly, pointing to Torrance.

"Objection!" Jeffries said. "The prosecutor indicated..."

"Objection denied," Colonel Goldsmith fired back.

"Thank you, Brenda." Donovan said, returning to his table. "Your witness, counsel."

Jeffries got up and gave Brenda a little smile as he walked over to her.

"You had a little problem for a minute picking out the right man, didn't you, Brenda?" Tony asked the question quietly as he stood and with a friendly voice.

"Yes, I guess I did. A little." There was a hint of a blush with her answer.

"There aren't a lot of Negroes who live in Oscoda, are there?"

"There aren't any. Except from the base."

"And there aren't many Negroes in the high school either, are there?"

"Not too many. Two, I think. No, three. There's a freshman girl. They're all from the base."

"Would you say that any of them are good friends of yours?"

"No. Not really." She glanced at Sergeant Marcus Jackson, seated at the far end of the court's table, then quickly looked back to Tony.

"So you don't socialize with any Negroes on a regular basis?"

"Oh, no," she said, shaking her head.

"Getting back to the problem you had a few minutes ago in picking out the defendant," Tony asked, "why do you suppose you had a little trouble in identifying the man you saw that night?"

169

"Well, probably because most Negro men look a lot alike," she answered.

When she saw that her answer brought whispered comments from the audience, Brenda raised her voice and added, "Everybody knows that."

"Thank you, Brenda."

At the left end of the court's table, Lieutenant John Kopecky turned and looked at Sergeant Jackson who rolled his eyes and shook his head.

Tony walked back to the defense table and picked up a large piece of white poster board that had been folded in half. As he leaned over, Wally whispered to him, "Can you believe she actually said that?"

Tony shook his head silently. Turning back to the witness, he said, "Now let's talk about that truck for a few minutes, Brenda."

"O.K." She sat confidently up on the front of her chair, crossing her legs. Every man in the courtroom noticed.

"How fast was it going when it passed you? Just approximately."

"Kinda fast for the road. Maybe twenty miles an hour. It's hard to say."

"I'm sure it is. But it was moving, wasn't it?"

"Oh, sure."

"And you and Bill were on the side road, outside the fence, facing in toward the Base, is that right?"

"Yes, that's right." She sat back a bit as she answered.

Tony sensed a sudden defensiveness in Brenda. She was probably afraid he was going to ask her *exactly* what

170

they were doing there. He was not going to ask her that.

"Did Bill have his car's headlights on?"

"I don't think so." She thought for a moment. "No, he didn't."

"And the truck passed directly in front of you, from left to right, as it drove along the base's perimeter road, is that right?"

"Yes."

"How far away was the truck when it passed in front of you?" he asked.

"Oh, I don't know. Maybe thirty or forty feet. I can't judge distances very well."

"I understand; neither can I sometimes." Tony smiled at her before continuing.

"Brenda, there are pine trees on both sides of that road that you and Bill were parked on, aren't there?"

"I guess so."

"So that, as you were looking forward, and that truck passed in front of you, you could only see it for a few seconds, isn't that right?"

"Well, we noticed it coming, because we could see its lights bumping up and down through the trees."

"But you only had a clear view of it when it passed in front of you, isn't that right?"

"That's right."

"Brenda, I'd like you to estimate how many seconds you could actually see that truck as it passed in front of you. And before you answer, I'd like you to look at the clock on the wall there." Tony pointed to the large clock at the back of the courtroom.

"I'd like you to watch the second hand on that clock, and at the same time recreate in your mind that truck driving past you. After you've done that, then tell us how many seconds you could see the truck clearly enough to identify it."

Brenda stared at the wall clock, running through the scene in her mind over and over again. Everyone in the room watched the clock's second hand slowly tick forward. Finally, Brenda looked back at Tony.

"Three or four seconds," she said.

"Thank you. And that was long enough for you to identify it as a Ford pickup?"

"Yes," she nodded as she answered. "There was a bright moon that night."

Tony unfolded the large piece of poster board he had been holding. It had a photograph of a pickup truck with a camper, clipped from a magazine ad, with pieces of paper taped over the name.

"Brenda, is this pickup truck a Ford or a Chevy?"

At that moment, Wally McDonald's metal pen rolled off the table hitting the tile floor. Tony had positioned himself so that the defense table was in Brenda's direct line of sight. Her eyes were momentarily diverted to the pen hitting the floor. When they returned to the picture of the truck, Tony snapped the poster board together.

"I'm sorry, could I see that again?" she asked with a smile.

"No, you can't, Brenda." Tony answered. "It was in

front of you for the same length of time that the truck passed in front of you on the night of January 8th, three or four seconds. Now, was the truck on the picture a Ford or a Chevy?"

She looked at Tony for several seconds. Her face was flushed and there was anger in her eyes.

"Come on, Brenda. Was it a Ford or a Chevy?"

Tom Donovan silently rose at the prosecutor's table, his eyes focused on Brenda.

The witness shut her eyes and concentrated. After a moment, she opened them, tossed her hair and looked at Tony confidently.

"It was a Ford."

Tony reopened the folded cardboard and slowly pulled off the taped paper covering the truck's make.

"I'm afraid not, Brenda. It's a Dodge."

"That's not fair," she exclaimed.

"I agree," Donovan added quickly. "That shabby trick was designed to confuse the witness. She should have been told that Dodge was a third alternative."

"Not at all," Tony responded. "On the night of January 8th there were dozens of possible alternatives. *She's* the one who identified it as a Ford. Maybe it was a Dodge that night too."

Tony strode over to the defense table, laid down the poster board, picked up several pieces of paper, laid one in front of Donovan and handed the rest to Colonel Grundig for distribution to the court and turned back to face the court.

"Gentlemen, I have here a Certificate from the Base Vehicle Registration Office stating that there are thirty-five Dodge pickup trucks registered to Wurtsmith personnel. Of those, eleven are equipped with campers and are owned by Negroes. This Certificate includes the names of those men. Since this witness clearly has some difficulty in distinguishing between Ford and Dodge pickups, this is highly relevant. We offer this Certificate as defense exhibit number one."

Donovan objected, but Colonel Goldsmith, after hesitating, said that as the Law Officer, he had no alternative but to admit the Certificate into evidence. Captain Jeffries had established its relevance.

"No further questions for this witness," Tony said. "Thank you Brenda."

Colonel Grundig recessed the proceedings for lunch at that point. Tony and Wally stood as everyone began milling around. Torrance didn't join them, but lit up a cigarette and stood with a small group of black Airmen who were watching the trial. The two AP guards were never far away.

"Tony, that was terrific!" Wally said. "You really hit a home run off her."

"We did all right, didn't we?" Tony smiled. He shared Wally's excitement on how well the cross-examination had gone. "Everything we tried, worked. We've still got a long way to go, though."

After lunch, Tom Donovan put Brenda Wendt back on the stand, and tried to rehabilitate her as a witness.

She insisted that Airman Torrance was in fact the man she saw that night, and that the vehicle she and Bill saw was definitely a Ford pickup.

Donovan allowed her to examine Jeffries' picture of a truck, and she was able to point out several differences between Fords and Dodges. She said she just didn't have enough time earlier to get a good look at the picture.

Donovan's last witness was Technical Sergeant Amos Watkins. He was black, in his late thirties, and wore two rows of military ribbons on the left side of his blue jacket. Sergeant Watkins testified that George Torrance had a terrible temper, and was vicious when he was drinking. He had seen several fights where other airmen had to intervene to prevent Torrance from seriously hurting or killing someone. Torrance had this habit, he said, of pulling a knife whenever he got angry, especially when he was drunk.

Torrance leaned back in his chair and stared hard at Sergeant Watkins as he testified. The witness kept his eyes on Donovan.

Tony objected to Watkins' testimony as being both prejudicial and irrelevant, but Colonel Goldsmith denied his objection.

On further cross-examination, Watkins admitted that barracks fights are not unusual, and that George Torrance may not be any meaner or more vicious than a number of other airmen.

As the witness was about to leave the stand, Sergeant Zeke Longtree spoke up from the end of the court's table.

"Colonel," he asked, addressing Colonel Grundig, "could I ask the witness a question or two?"

"Go ahead, sergeant."

"As a matter of fact, Sergeant Watkins," Longtree asked, "you've been known to engage in a few barracks fights yourself, haven't you?" There was a friendly tone to the question.

"Why, yes, I believe I have." He smiled in return.

"Have you ever pulled a knife or another weapon in one of those barrack fights?"

Watkins paused, "I guess I may have, once or twice."

"Does that mean that you're a dangerous man, Sergeant"?

"Not necessarily, Sergeant Longtree."

Longtree nodded and leaned back. "That's all, Colonel," he said. The two sergeants exchanged a glance and Colonel Grundig told the witness he was excused. He stood, saluted the court, turned and strode from the room.

"Anything further for the prosecution, Captain Donovan?" Colonel Grundig asked.

Donovan rummaged through the papers on his table, opened his trial bag and lifted out a stack of photographs. He looked concerned.

"Yes, there is," he said. "I intend to formally introduce into evidence a number of the items that were identified earlier by several of the witnesses. I'm having a bit of a problem, though, and would appreciate the court's indulgence."

"Fine," Colonel Grundig said. "Take your time, Captain."

Grundig emptied his pipe into an ashtray, tapping it several times to clean it out. He opened his tobacco pouch and very deliberately refilled his pipe. He tamped it down when he was through, struck a match, relit, and puffed on his pipe. As the cloud of gray haze enveloped him, Colonel Grundig leaned back and looked at the prosecutor.

Donovan continued going through his documents and exhibits, including those being held in the exhibit box. He was looking for something. He lifted his trial bag onto the table and dug into it. He went over to Ruth Olmsted and asked her a question. She shook her head.

Donovan walked back to his table, cleared his throat, and looked up at the court.

"Gentlemen," he said, "There are a number of exhibits I'd like to formally introduce into evidence at this time. They've all been previously identified by various witnesses. However, there is one item of evidence I can't seem to find."

"What is that, Captain Donovan?" Grundig asked.

"The wristwatch found in Laurie McAllister's house by Major Pawlowski," Donovan answered. "It was identified and tagged, but not tendered for admission at the time. It's been with our exhibits throughout the trial, but it's gone now. I have no idea where it is."

A wave of whispered comments swept the courtroom. The men on the court began exchanging quiet remarks. Colonel Grundig brought back order with a bang of his gavel.

"Well, that's unfortunate, but not a serious problem,"

Grundig said. "Major Pawlowski told us how he found the watch, and identified it in court. He also testified about the initials engraved on the back. So that evidence is already in the record."

"Just a minute," Tony said, rising. "The defense was never given the opportunity to examine that watch. We don't know that there are initials engraved on the back of it. Neither do the members of the court. If the watch isn't going to be tendered as an exhibit, we move that all the testimony regarding that watch be stricken."

"That's not appropriate at all," Donovan snapped. "Major Pawlowski's testimony stands on its own. He told the court what he found and he identified that watch with its engraving in the course of his direct examination."

"I agree," Colonel Goldsmith said. "The defense motion to strike is denied. Major Pawlowski's testimony regarding the watch will remain of record. Unfortunately, however, the watch itself will apparently not be an exhibit."

"Son-of-a-bitch!" Tony whispered to McDonald as he sat down. "Do you suppose the watch was a fake, and they lost it on purpose? Maybe the watch we saw for a second in court was a Timex they bought that morning at the Base Exchange."

"Could be. Now they've got the benefit of the damn incriminating watch in the record, without an actual watch."

Goldsmith admitted the remainder of Donovan's exhibits into evidence, and the prosecution rested.

Colonel Grundig looked at the clock on the wall, said the court would recess for fifteen minutes, until three o'clock when the defense would be expected to begin presenting its case.

"We scored some points, George, but we're still way behind," Tony said to Torrance after the court had recessed and stepped out. "And this phantom watch irritates the hell out of me."

"I know'd they din't have no goddamn watch with my initials on it, cap'n," Torrance sneered. "I've never owned a watch like that." He turned and walked out to the hallway, followed closely by the two AP's with their automatic rifles.

"In a way, I'm glad the watch vanished," McDonald said quietly to Tony. "That was the one piece of evidence that we couldn't explain away. The fact that it doesn't exist really confirms George's story."

"That's right," Tony answered. "But we have to convince the court of that."

Chapter 13

—*mm*—

"The defense calls Miss Lucy Jenks as its first witness."

Tony waited while Wally escorted Lucy Jenks to the witness stand; she smiled nervously at Tony as she passed the defense table. She was dressed in a trim navy blue suit with a white blouse and was carrying a small cloth purse in her left hand. After she was sworn in and seated, she glanced toward the crowded courtroom. Her eyes met George Torrance's briefly, but neither showed any reaction.

"Would you state your name please?" Tony asked.

He was holding his yellow pad of notes and standing at the far end of the court's long table, facing the witness. That was where Bob Cunningham had suggested he stand. In responding to Tony, the witnesses would appear to be speaking directly to the court.

"Lucy Jenks," she answered softly.

"Where do you reside, Miss Jenks?"

"In Saginaw."

"What's your present business or occupation, Miss Jenks?"

"I'm a waitress at the Esquire Restaurant in Saginaw., I jus' began last week."

"Do you know the defendant in this case, Airman George Torrance?"

"Yes sir, I do." She glanced quickly toward Torrance as she answered.

"Would it be fair to say, Miss Jenks, that you are George Torrance's girlfriend?" Tony smiled as he asked the question.

"Yes, sir. We've talked about gettin' married some-day." She returned Tony's smile, and looked at Torrance again. He nodded and let a slight smile cross his face.

"I take it, Miss Jenks, that you and George Torrance see a lot of each other on a regular basis."

"Oh yes. Least we did before all this happened." She gestured toward the court with her left hand.

"I understand. Tell me, Miss Jenks, where were you on the night of this past January 8th?"

"I was with George," she answered with her chin raised slightly. Her answer was firm but her voice was so soft that Tony wasn't sure everyone had heard it.

"You were with the defendant, George Torrance?"

"Yes sir, I was."

"Would you tell us about it please?"

"Well, I drove up from Saginaw and got to Oscoda 'bout seven. George wasn't workin' that day. When I got to the Shell station I called George, like I always do. After I told him I was here I drove round to that gate on the back side. By the time I got there, George had already opened the gate and was waitin' in his pickup. So I just drove right in."

"Were there any air policemen there that night, Miss Jenks?" Tony asked. "At the back gate?"

"No, 'course not," she smiled. "That's the whole idea. We didn't want them to know I came in."

"Why not?"

"Because I was gonna spend the night, and single women ain't supposed to spend the night on Base," she replied, looking down at the purse in her lap.

Tony asked, "May I call you Lucy?"

"Course," she answered, looking up with a smile.

Out on the tarmac, one of the B-52s turned on its engines. The noise rose steadily, rattling the panes of glass in the courtroom's windows. Tony waited while the plane taxied to the main runway, then began its long takeoff.

"What happened next, Lucy, after you came in through the back gate?" he asked, raising his voice over the fading aircraft engines.

"Well, after George shut the gate again, he got in his pickup and I followed him 'round that road to the barracks. We both parked in back. George had some chicken and two bottles of wine in his room, and we stayed there 'til the next mornin." Lucy's voice trailed off and she looked down again as she finished.

"What time did you leave the next day, Lucy?" Tony

was trying to keep his voice as friendly and reassuring as possible.

"'Bout nine. It was already light."

"And how did you leave that next morning?"

"Same way I got in," she answered. "George let me out the back gate."

"Is it your testimony, Lucy, that you were with George Torrance the entire time from a little after seven on the night of January 8th, until nine o'clock on the morning of January 9th?" Tony asked.

"No sir," she said quietly.

Tony froze. "Pardon me?"

"No sir, he went to the bathroom a couple of times. I did too." A wave of muffled laughter swept the room. She glanced at George Torrance and they both smiled.

Tony's momentary panic subsided. Tony paused a moment, before going on.

"Lucy, are you sure it was the night of January 8th you were with George Torrance?"

"Yes, I am."

"How can you be so sure it was that particular night?"

"Cuz it's my birthday. George wanted to be with me to give me a present."

"Did he give you a present that night, Lucy?"

"Yes, he gave me these." She smiled and pulled her hair back on the left side, showing a pearl earring. Then she did the same on the right side. "These earrings."

"Lucy, do you have anything with you to prove that January 8th is your birthday?"

"Yes sir, I do." She opened her purse, pulled out a piece of plastic, and handed it to Tony. "My driver's license."

Tony took the license, showed it to Captain Donovan, then handed it to Colonel Grundig. As the men on the court passed the license around, they all saw that Lucy Jenks' birthday was in fact January 8th. A photocopy of the license was admitted as defense exhibit two.

Tony concluded by asking the witness what sort of a man George Torrance was.

She looked directly at George as she answered. "He's the warmest, most gentle man I've ever known." Her eyes were moist when she looked back to Tony.

"Colonel," Tony said, turning to the Presiding Officer. "I'd like to move to admit all the defense exhibits as they're identified in this testimony; rather than as a group at the close of our case, with the Court's consent."

"No objection," Donovan responded without even looking up.

"Hearing no objection," Grundig ruled, "the defense motion is granted."

"Your witness, counsel," Tony said to Tom Donovan. *Here comes the test.*

Donovan stood and looked at Lucy a long time; long enough to make her shift uncomfortably in her seat.

Finally, he slowly walked over to her.

"The Air Police don't have any record of your car being on base that night, Miss Jenks. You know that, don't you?"

"Yes, sir. That's cuz George let me in and out the back gate." She was still looking down, speaking quietly.

"Tell us again, Miss Jenks," Donovan asked, "Why did you use the maintenance gate when you came on the Base that night?"

"So George wouldn't get in trouble."

"What do you mean by that?" The room was completely quiet now. Every eye was on Donovan and the witness.

"Well, like I said to Cap'n Jeffries, women ain't supposed to spend the night in the barracks."

"How do you know that?"

"George tol' me."

"Did you know that no one's supposed to use that gate when it's locked at night?"

"Yes, sir. George tol' me that too."

Donovan was moving around the courtroom now as he asked his questions. He reminded Tony of a lion stalking a defenseless prey.

"So you knew that it was against Air Force regulations for you to spend the night on base, and you knew it was against regulations to come in at night through the maintenance gate, is that right?" Donovan asked.

"Yes, sir." Lucy answered softly.

"And you did both of those things, because George Torrance wanted you to do them, isn't that right?"

"Yes, sir."

"You'd do just about anything that George asked you to do, wouldn't you, Lucy?"

"Well, maybe so, sir." Her voice was so soft it was hardly audible.

"I'm sorry, Miss Jenks, but you're going to have to speak up," Donovan said. "I don't believe the court heard your last answer. I asked whether it was true that you'd do just about anything that George Torrance asked you to do. Would you repeat your answer, please?"

"Yes, sir," she answered, only slightly louder. "I probably would." Several men on the court scribbled notes.

"And if George Torrance asked you to lie to this court by saying you were with him that night, and you really weren't, you'd do that too, wouldn't you?"

"Why, no sir," Lucy stammered.

"Come now, Miss Jenks, you knew George Torrance was a married man, didn't you?"

"Yes, sir, I did."

"But that didn't stop you from *fornicating* with him on a regular basis, did it?" Donovan spat the question out like a revival preacher.

She looked at him in shock, her eyes open wide.

"Objection!" Tony shouted.

"Denied." Colonel Goldsmith fired back.

George Torrance started to rise, his fists clenched. Wally forcefully pulled him back down into his seat as the two AP's started to move forward.

Lucy appeared flustered, not knowing how to respond. Before she could, Donovan pressed on.

"You broke every rule in the book for George Torrance, Miss Jenks. You've already confessed to that.

Is there any reason on earth why you wouldn't break one more for him and perjure yourself here?" Donovan thundered out his question.

Tears welled up in Lucy's eyes. She didn't answer.

"I didn't think you could respond to that question, Miss Jenks," Donovan said as he returned to his table and sat down. "No further questions are necessary."

"Jesus, he really cut her up," McDonald whispered.

"Yeah, I know."

Lucy looked crushed. Her shoulders sagged, and she stared down at a handkerchief she was fumbling to take out of her purse. Tony wanted to walk up to her, put his arm around Lucy, and assure her that everything was all right. But he couldn't; and everything *wasn't* all right. The best he could do was to ask her a few gentle follow-up questions to help her regain her composure.

"Lucy, all of Captain Donovan's bullying aside, you were with George Torrance the entire night...," Tony started to ask.

"Objection!" Donovan shouted, knocking his chair over backward as he jumped to his feet. "There's been no bullying here. Just an effort to clean up some obvious perjury that the defense is trying to foist on the court, and probably committing more perjury in the process. It's perfectly clear that this witness didn't give us a single truthful answer after her name. And if we checked into that, we'd probably find that to be a lie, too!"

Tony started to respond to Donovan's outburst, but was cut off by the Law Officer, Colonel Goldsmith.

"The prosecutor's objection is sustained," he ruled. "Captain Jeffries, I caution you to be more prudent in your choice of language."

Tony looked over at Lucy. She was sobbing softly, holding her handkerchief to her eyes. He had more questions he was prepared to ask, but was afraid that she couldn't stand up to the cross that would eventually follow. There was no point in asking her anything more.

"No further questions," Tony said quietly as he sat down.

Colonel Grundig told Lucy that she was excused. She held her hankie to her face as she ran from the courtroom, avoiding George's eyes.

———

Carl Schroeder was having dinner at his usual table in the Redwood Lodge when Major Jimmy Davis walked in. The special that day was chili; its spicy aroma filled the dining room. There were only half-a-dozen other diners there.

Davis hung up his coat, kicked the snow from his boots, pulled up a chair and sat down across from the white-haired mayor. Caroline Schroeder gave him a cheerful greeting as she brought another glass of water and a dog-eared menu to the table.

"I hear you've had a few problems in the trial," Mayor Schroeder said without looking up.

"A few," Davis responded. "But nothing serious. This

defense counsel, Jeffries, is being a real asshole. He's taking his job much too seriously."

Carl Schroeder put his spoon down and stared hard at Major Davis. "I want to remind you," he said slowly and forcefully, "that you gave me a firm commitment about this trial. If it wasn't for that, I wouldn't have waived civil jurisdiction, and this case would be tried before Judge Palmer in Tawas City." He kept his eyes on Davis as he raised his cup and took a sip of coffee. "Do you recall that conversation we had?"

"Yes, sir, I certainly do," Davis replied quietly, his eyes locked on the mayor's. "And we intend to live up to our commitment."

"I'm holding you and the Wing Commander to that," Schroeder continued, quietly, but with a steely firmness in his voice. "If you don't deliver, I can assure you that both the Air Force and the two of you personally are going to have some serious problems. Serious problems! In case you're not aware of it, the congressman from this district is my cousin. And he sits on the Armed Services Committee."

"Don't worry, Mr. Mayor. We have certain things in mind that we intend to implement. We're not going to let this case get away from us."

"I certainly hope you're right, Major Davis, for everyone's sake."

—*mm*—

Late that night, eighty miles to the south in Saginaw, a young woman lay on her bed in a darkened room over the Esquire Restaurant. Her body was racked with spasms of uncontrollable sobbing.

Lucy Jenks hadn't been able to stop crying since Captain Donovan assaulted her during the trial that afternoon. She had to pull off the road four times on the way back in order to get control of herself. George was so important to her; but now, all this. She had tried to help her man, but had only made things worse.

Chapter 14

George Torrance was nervous as he took the stand the next morning. He tried not to show it, but it was clear to Tony by the way his eyes darted around the courtroom. They had decided that the best, and perhaps only, way to defeat the prosecution's case was for George to stand up to Tom Donovan's expected intensive cross-examination. Tony and Wally had read that conventional criminal defense theory was the opposite; that unless the prosecution met its burden of overcoming the presumption of the defendant's innocence, a finding of "not guilty" had to be made and, as a general rule, the defendant shouldn't be put on the stand. But they felt that presumption probably didn't exist in this case and under these circumstances, behind the closed walls of a Court Martial, on a remote SAC Base and so they resolved that Torrance would take the stand to testify in his own defense. Torrance agreed.

"Airman Torrance," Tony began, after the witness had been sworn, "Where are you from originally?"

"Macon, Georgia, sir," Torrance answered. He looked good in his freshly pressed uniform. A row of ribbons on his chest reminded everyone that he was a career Airman.

"Were you drafted into the Air Force, Airman Torrance, or did you enlist?" Tony asked.

"I enlisted, sir. 1 September, 1955."

"And what was the first base to which you were assigned?"

"Lackland, sir; in Texas. Then Wright-Patt in Ohio for 'lectronics school."

"So you've been in the Air Force thirteen years, is that correct?"

"Yes, sir, it is."

"I understand that you're an electronics technician, is that correct?"

"Yes, sir. I've been to all three 'lectronics schools," Torrance answered, sitting erect and totally focused on Tony. "I know every inch of wiring inside a B-52, sir." There was pride in the man's voice.

Tony asked Torrance some more questions about his background in the service and the bases he'd been assigned to. Torrance replied that his last base, before Wurtsmith, was Bitburg in Germany.

When it came to the events of January 8th, Torrance's testimony closely paralleled that of Lucy Jenks'. He related he let Lucy in and out through the unmanned south gate in order to get around the regulation that prohibits single women from spending the night in the barracks. He added that airmen commonly let their girlfriends in that way.

On the left side of the court's table, Captain Fanzone gave an inquiring glance to Sergeant Longtree beside him. Longtree shrugged his shoulders. It wasn't *that* common.

"Airman Torrance," Tony went on, "I'd like to direct your attention now to the early morning hours of January 29th. Will you tell the court what you did that night?"

"Yes, sir." Torrance shifted slightly so that he was facing the court directly. "I was workin' the second shift that day. My usual shift. We got out 'bout midnight, and I drove over to Blake's in my pickup. That's what all of us do every night. I was there until it closed about 5 in the mornin'."

"What were you doing during that period of time?" Tony asked.

"I had a steak sandwich and a bunch of beers." Torrance shrugged his shoulders. "Same thin' I have every night."

"Can you tell us, Airman Torrance, some of the men who were with you there at Blake's on the night of January 28th and early morning on the 29th?"

"Sure. The guys who are usually there are..."

"Objection," Donovan said, rising to his feet. "It doesn't really matter who is *usually* there. The only relevant question is who was there that *particular* night."

"Objection sustained," Colonel Goldsmith ruled.

Tony decided to rephrase the question.

"Airman Torrance" he asked, "will you tell us who you can specifically recall being there that night."

"Well, Cap'n," Torrance replied, "there are certain

193

guys who are there jus' 'bout every night. Guys like Scratch, Juice, Buddha...,"

"Just a minute." Tom Donovan was on his feet again. "I object to this testimony unless the witness is going to state, under oath, that these particular men were in fact there on the night of January 29th. He should not be allowed to speculate about who *might* have been there."

"I agree. The objection is sustained," Goldsmith quickly stated. "The defendant's previous testimony about who is *usually* at Blake's will be stricken." Speaking to Torrance directly, Goldsmith added, "Airman Torrance, can you state for certain who was there that night?"

"You mean absolutely, Colonel?"

"That's what I'm asking you."

"No, sir, I don't think I can do that. But I can tell you who's there jus' 'bout every night. So most of them would be there that night for sure."

"I'm afraid that's not good enough," Goldsmith responded. "Any further speculative testimony by the defendant along these lines will be immediately stricken. Proceed, Captain Jeffries."

Tony didn't like the way that went. He had Torrance reconfirm the fact that he had been there all night, then decided to move on to another area.

"Airman Torrance, what time is it?" Tony asked as casually as he could.

Torrance glanced at his watch, then looked up with some confusion. "Why, its oh-ten-thirty, sir.

"May I see your watch, please."

Torrance unfastened the leather band, took off his watch and handed it to Tony.

"How long have you owned this watch, Airman Torrance?"

"'Bout three years, sir. I bought it in Stuttgart when I's stationed in Germany. I've worn it ever since."

After showing the watch to Captain Donovan, Tony handed it to Colonel Grundig. "I would like the court to note that this is a Broche watch, it's German-made, and the leather band shows some signs of wear," He added "It certainly appears to be the watch that Airman Torrance has probably been wearing for the past three years. I would also note that there's nothing engraved on the back."

After every man on the court had an opportunity to look at the watch, Tony took it back and returned it to the witness.

"Airman Torrance," Tony asked. "Have you ever owned a watch with your initials engraved on the back?"

"No, sir. Never. That's somethin' a woman would do, sir."

Tony walked to the far side of the courtroom, turned and faced the defendant.

"Airman Torrance, did you murder and rape Peggy Wilton?" The punch of the question caught everyone's attention.

"No, sir. I did not."

"Did you murder and rape Laurie McAllister?"

"No, sir."

The reporters again began scribbling notes. There was

more whispering as Tony paused.

Tony turned to the court. "Gentlemen," he said, "that completes our examination of the defendant. We are prepared to turn him over to the prosecutor for cross-examination in a moment. Before doing so, however, we would like to conduct a brief demonstration."

"What do you mean, Captain Jeffries?" Colonel Grundig asked.

"I'm fully aware of the fact that the defendant's credibility is a major factor in this case," Tony answered. Several men on the court nodded their concurrence.

As Tony spoke, he walked to the front of the court's table. "If you believe Airman Torrance's testimony," he said, "you have to find him not guilty. On the other hand, if you don't believe him, you might very well find Airman Torrance guilty as charged. Whether George Torrance is truthful or not is the central issue in this case. I would like to do something that will prove to you that George Torrance is a believable, credible person and that you should believe his testimony."

"What do you have in mind, Captain? A polygraph test?" Grundig asked.

"No, sir. Polygraph results aren't admissible as evidence. What I have in mind is this. Airman Torrance has testified that he let Miss Jenks in the south gate on January 8th and out again the next morning, and that he knows how to open the lock on that gate without a key. Some of you might find that testimony to be unbelievable and purely self-serving."

"That's exactly right, Captain," Major Smithfield cut in. "The Air Force spends a great deal of money on its security systems, especially at a base like this, and I don't believe for a moment that Airman Torrance or anyone else, except maybe a locksmith, can just open that gate at will."

"Major, if we could prove to you that Airman Torrance is telling the truth on this one particular point, would that make his overall testimony more credible in your eyes?" Tony asked.

"Yes, I suppose it might," Smithfield responded.

"Then, gentlemen, I propose that all of us, the entire court, go out to the south perimeter fence of the base right now and see if Airman Torrance can open that maintenance gate as he has testified."

Tony's proposition caught everyone by surprise.

"I don't think that's at all necessary," Donovan answered, rising slowly. "The men on the court can rely on their own judgment and experience to know that security locks can't be opened without keys or other special tools. Unless you cut them, of course. There's really no need for us all to troop out to the south fence."

"May I comment on that, Colonel?" Bolte asked, addressing the president. Grundig felt uneasy cutting off the discussion since Bolte, as a squadron commander, was one of the more important officers on base. "Go ahead, Colonel Bolte," he responded after a pause.

"Thank you. On the other hand," Colonel Bolte said, "if Torrance *can* do it, that does give his credibility a boost. It would also mean that we have a serious security problem."

"Colonel, don't misunderstand me," Donovan said, standing at the prosecutor's table. "I have no objection to the court going out right now to check Airman Torrance's story. I just think it will be a complete waste of time." As he finished, Donovan looked directly at Colonel Bolte.

"Well, I'd like to see whether Airman Torrance can open that gate or not," Colonel Bolte answered.

"So would I," Captain Fanzone added.

Everyone else acquiesced, and Colonel Grundig recessed the court with instructions that they would reconvene in fifteen minutes at the south maintenance gate. The Air Police would take the defendant, he added.

The courtroom emptied to a rising buzz of conversation. Spectators who were without cars quickly sought rides. Within moments, a convoy of thirty to forty vehicles snaked its way out of the parking lot and began moving westward along the south perimeter fence. It was a dark overcast day, and the low cloud ceiling threatened to lay even more snow on top of the deep base that already covered Wurtsmith. Tony and McDonald rode in Wally's Plymouth, followed closely by an enclosed jeep with Torrance and three armed AP's. They all came to a halt on the south side of the base, adjacent to the maintenance gate in the outer fence. The deep snow on both sides prevented anyone from pulling their car off the road.

"It doesn't look like anyone's used this gate since the blizzard," Tony said quietly to Wally as they got out of the car and trudged up the drift on the left side of the road. There were no tire tracks between the maintenance gate and the road. It would have been impossible for most vehicles to drive through that snow.

The crowd lumbered through the snow and formed a rough half-circle around the gate. Sixty to seventy people were there. The court reporter, Ruth Olmsted, was trying to figure out how to hold her steno pad and pen with her mittened hands. She had decided to record this proceeding in shorthand.

"All right, Captain Jeffries," Colonel Grundig said, raising his voice above the icy north wind. "The court is reconvened. What do you want to show us?"

"I'd like Airman Torrance to show you how he opened this gate on the night of January 8th, when he let Lucy Jenks onto the base." Turning to Torrance, Tony nodded.

George Torrance walked through the deep snow to the gate, grabbed the lock and turned it so that it faced the adjacent metal pole. He stepped back a pace, raised his foot and gave the lock a hard kick.

Nothing happened.

"Son of a bitch," Torrance muttered.

He kicked it a second time, harder. Again, nothing happened. Torrance walked up to the lock and yanked it. It didn't budge. He glanced back at Tony, then kicked it one more time. Nothing.

"That's what I thought," Captain Donovan said with a smirk. "I want the record to reflect the fact that Airman Torrance has attempted to open the lock on this gate, and has failed. Several times. Colonel, I suggest that we get out of here, and resume this trial in a proper courtroom."

"I agree," Grundig answered. "Let's go."

"What in the hell happened?" McDonald asked Tony. "We saw it work just the other day."

"I don't know what happened, Cap'n," Torrance said to Tony, his voice reflecting both confusion and apology. Two air policemen grabbed Torrance's arms before Tony could reply and began leading him back toward the road. The crowd, gathered in small clusters, was laughing and looking over their shoulders at Torrance as he was forcefully marched back to the road.

"What a bunch of bullshit," somebody muttered.

"I don't understand it either," Tony said to Wally. "I'm going to take a look at that lock."

He walked up to the gate, pulled a piece of folded yellow paper out of his coat pocket, and held the lock in his hand. *The serial number was different!* He looked up and saw Sergeant Dahlke, ten feet away, watching him closely. Dahlke was nervously fingering the strap of his automatic rifle, which was slung over his shoulder.

"Colonel Grundig," Tony shouted. Everyone stopped and turned back. "Colonel, I want to show something to you and the rest of the court. This is important."

Grundig hesitated. "All right," he said, returning to the gate. "It better be. We're reconvened, for the moment." Ruth Olmsted dug her steno pad and pen from her shoulder bag as she trudged back to the gate.

With the court at the gate, Tony held up the piece of

yellow paper he had been holding.

"Gentlemen," he said, raising his voice. "This is the serial number of the lock that was on this gate four days ago. Airman Torrance demonstrated to us that he could, in fact, kick open the lock. I wrote this number down that night. *This* lock," he said, pointing to the one on the gate, "has a different number. It's M-031. The lock has been changed in the last four days."

The court members began exchanging whispered comments. Finally, Colonel Bolte spoke up.

"Captain Jeffries, are you saying that you saw Airman Torrance open this gate four days ago by kicking the lock? The way he tried today?"

"Yes, sir. I am."

"Who else was present?"

"Just Lieutenant McDonald and Sergeant Dahlke," Tony said, nodding to the air policeman. "The sergeant escorted Torrance out here that night."

Colonel Bolte turned to Dahlke. "Sergeant, has this lock been changed in the past four days?"

"No, sir. Not at far as I know, sir," he answered.

"That's easy enough to find out," Bolte responded. "Captain Jeffries, what's the number on the lock there? The lock on the gate."

"M-031," Tony answered.

"Kopecky, get on your radio," Colonel Bolte barked. "Tell the top sergeant in the Quartermaster's Office to meet us back at the HQ in fifteen minutes. Have him bring the records of lock M-031 with him. Understand?"

"Yes, sir." Lieutenant Kopecky turned and strode back through the snow to the line of parked cars.

"I'm sorry, Colonel," Bolte commented to Colonel Grundig, who was standing beside him. "I assume that this is all right with you?"

"Yes, of course," Grundig muttered as he turned and walked back toward his car.

—*mm*—

Master Sergeant Paul Wong was the NCO in charge of Wurtsmith Quartermaster's Shop. He was dressed in his fatigues, waiting for the court when the caravan returned from the south perimeter fence. Sergeant Wong was a tall chunky Hawaiian who always seemed out of place in snow-covered northern Michigan.

He was sworn in as the court's own witness; as everyone was hanging their overcoats over the backs of their chairs. After all the court members had taken their usual seats, Colonel Bolte began asking questions, with Colonel Grundig's consent.

"Sergeant Wong, do you have your records for lock M-031 with you?"

"Yes, sir, right here sir," he answered, holding up a thin manila folder.

"When was that lock issued out of your shop?" Bolte asked.

Wong opened his folder, and glanced at the single sheet of paper inside.

"Yesterday, sir," he answered.

"And who was it issued to, Sergeant?"

"Sergeant Dahlke of the Air Police, Colonel."

Mike Bolte leaned back in his chair and said nothing for a moment. His eyes swept the courtroom. Dahlke wasn't there. When he resumed speaking, leaning forward, barely controlled rage showed in his voice.

"Did Sergeant Dahlke tell you why he wanted the lock yesterday, Sergeant Wong?"

"Yes, sir. He said they had to replace a lock on the south maintenance gate. He said it wasn't working properly."

"He said that to you personally?"

"Yes, sir."

"Thank you, sergeant," Colonel Bolte was through. He folded his aims and stared at the prosecutor, Tom Donovan.

"Does anyone else have any questions for Sergeant Wong?" Colonel Grundig asked, reasserting his prerogative as President of the Court. Everyone at the long table shook their heads in the negative.

"No questions," Donovan answered, looking down as he rearranged some papers on his desk.

A thought struck Tony. "I have a question," he said, rising slowly.

"Go ahead, Captain," Colonel Grundig replied.

"Sergeant, whatever happened to the old lock that was on the south gate?"

"Why, it's right here, sir," Wong said, pulling a steel

lock out of the right pocket of his fatigues. "Sergeant Dahlke brought it back to us last night."

"Beautiful." Wally whispered.

Tony walked over to the witness chair. "May I see it, please?" Sergeant Wong handed the lock to him.

Tony took the lock and laid it on the tile floor, face down. He lifted his right foot and slammed his heel down on the lock.

It popped open.

He picked up the opened lock, walked over to the Court's table, and laid it in front of Major Smithfield. Pointing to the serial number engraved in the lock's base, Tony said, "We submit lock number A-655 as defense exhibit three."

Tony confidently pulled the piece of yellow paper from his inner coat pocket, unfolded it, and laid it next to the lock in front of Major Smithfield. "And we submit this as defense exhibit four, my note showing the serial number of the lock on the south gate four days ago."

The number A-655 on the paper was circled in red.

Chapter 15

—·mm·—

At eleven o'clock that morning, February 28th, Wurtsmith's Command Post received a telex from SAC Headquarters at Offut Air Force Base. The first two squadrons of the 379th Bomb Wing were being ordered to Guam. There, the planes' bomb bays would be reconfigured to carry iron bombs rather than nuclear weapons; their mission was to conduct tactical bombing of the Ho Chi Minh Trail. The message was delivered to Lieutenant Colonel Grundig presiding over Airman Torrance's court martial at 11:15 a.m. and he declared an early lunch recess. Within an hour, everyone on base knew that half the wing would be pulling out the following Sunday, March 3rd.

Lieutenant Colonel Michael Bolte's squadron was one of those being sent to Guam. It was essential now to bring the court martial of Airman Torrance to a rapid conclusion.

—*mm*—

Donovan's cross-examination of George Torrance was the first order of business when the court reconvened after lunch. He stood in front of the prosecution's table, thumbing silently through Torrance's military personnel folder, until he had the attention of everyone in the courtroom. When he did, he looked up at the defendant.

"You've had a few problems in the Air Force haven't you, Airman Torrance?" It was a statement, not a question.

"Yes, sir. I've had my fair share of problems."

"Oh, I think you're being modest, Torrance," Donovan smiled. "You've had far more than your *fair share*. You've had enough problems for an entire squadron; perhaps a whole wing. Isn't that right, Airman Torrance?"

"Well, maybe so, sir."

Tony rose to his feet. "Gentlemen, I've got to object to this line of questioning. Any past difficulties which the defendant may have had are totally irrelevant to the question of whether he's guilty or innocent of the charges before this court."

"Quite to the contrary," Donovan retorted. "When the defendant took the stand in his own defense he put his veracity in issue. Defense counsel himself said that Airman Torrance's credibility was the central issue in this trial. That being the case, the court is certainly entitled to have Airman Torrance's entire military record before it in order to evaluate his credibility."

"I agree," Colonel Goldsmith said. "The defense objection is denied. Proceed, Captain Donovan."

McDonald leaned over to Tony. "Nice try," he whispered. "We've seen George's record. Donovan's going to kill us with it."

"I know," Tony answered.

"Let's see," Donovan said as he continued thumbing through the papers in Torrance's file. "You were convicted by a Special Court Martial of theft in 1958, and reduced to Airman Basic. Isn't that right?"

"Yes, sir."

"And it looks like you were court martialed again and convicted in 1962. This time for striking a non-commissioned officer. Reduced to Airman Basic again. Is that correct?"

"Yes, sir."

"Well, this is interesting, Airman Torrance," Donovan said, scratching his head. "It seems as though you threatened the NCO with a knife in that case. The charges ended up being reduced to simple assault by a plea bargain. Is that correct?"

"Again, I object," Tony said rising quickly to his feet. "Airman Torrance is being charged here with four felonies. Any possible misdemeanors he may or may not have committed in the past are totally inadmissible."

"I've already ruled on that Captain Jeffries," Colonel Goldsmith responded sternly. "Now sit down!" Tony slowly obliged.

"Airman Torrance," Grundig raised his voice. "Please

answer Captain Donovan's question."

"Ah, well, you see, sir..."

"Yes or no, Torrance," Donovan fired back. "Were you charged with threatening an NCO with a knife in that case or not?"

"Yes, sir." Torrance looked down at the floor.

"It also seems, Airman Torrance, that you received a few disciplinary actions under Article 15. How many do we have here?" he asked himself aloud as he flipped through the pages in Torrance's file. "Three? Four? Five? Wait, here's one more. Six! Is that right, Airman Torrance? You've been disciplined six times under Article 15?"

"Yes, sir," Torrance answered, slumping down in his chair.

"I'd say you were being *very* modest before, Airman Torrance," Donovan continued. "You've had far more than your fair share of problems. In fact, what amazes me, Airman Torrance, is that you managed to stay in the Air Force at all with your *fair share* of problems."

Tony rose to his feet.

"Is that a question, Captain Donovan, or are you slipping into your closing argument here?" Tony said. Turning to Colonel Goldsmith, he added, "I object to the prosecutor's harassing the defendant like this. These aren't legitimate questions."

"Objection denied," Goldsmith answered impassively.

Donovan continued thumbing through Torrance's file while he waited for Tony to sit down. He pulled a page out and looked up at the defendant. "Have you ever had any nicknames, Airman Torrance?" he asked.

"A few, sir," Torrance shrugged. "Different people call you different things."

"How about 'Slasher'?" Donovan asked. "Has that ever been a nickname of yours?"

"At my last base, yes sir."

"Did you get the nickname Slasher because of an incident with a group of civilians in Bitburg where three young Germans were cut up a bit?"

"Yes, sir. I believe so."

"All right, Slasher, excuse me, Airman Torrance, let's talk now about the incidents that occurred here this past January, a little over a month ago, where a couple of other people got cut up a bit," Donovan slowly walked toward Torrance as he spoke. "Tell us again what your story is for the night of January 8th."

Torrance repeated his prior testimony about being with Lucy Jenks the entire night, only this time Donovan was interrupting, contradicting, and challenging him every step of the way. Every time Tony raised an objection, it was summarily denied by Colonel Goldsmith.

Then Donovan concentrated on the events surrounding Laurie McAllister's killing. He was relentless and brutal in his questioning, hammering away at the fact that Torrance had absolutely no corroboration for his alibi that he arrived at Blake's that night.

Donovan ended his cross-examination a little after three, and Colonel Grundig declared a fifteen minute recess. When Torrance returned to the defense table Tony could see that he was soaking with perspiration. Tony suggested that they step out for some coffee during the break.

Jeffries and McDonald got coffee from the vending machine down the hall from the courtroom. Torrance said he preferred something cold, and got a coke. The two armed air police guards had followed Torrance out of the courtroom, but Tony insisted that they stand far enough away for he and Wally to be able to discuss the case privately with their client. They stepped back.

"George, do you want to go back on the stand?" Tony asked as he stirred some powdered cream substitute into his coffee. "We're entitled to redirect; I could have you reestablish your alibis. There might be some value in that."

"Then Cap'n Donovan would be entitled to cross-examine me again. Ain't that right?"

"That's right, George," Tony responded.

"No, man. I don't want no more of that fucker. I'm done."

"OK, George. It's your call," Tony said. Looking to Wally, he added, "That's it, then. We don't have any more witnesses. When we go back in, we'll have to rest. Isn't that the way you see it, Wally?"

"That's right," McDonald responded, tossing his paper cup into a metal waste basket, looking the defendant straight in the eyes. "We've played all the cards we've got. I'm not sure that's going to be enough, though. You know that, George."

"I know Cap'n," George Torrance said quietly. He stared at his bottle of slowly swirling Coke. "I know'd that from the start. There wasn't nothin' you two coulda done to change things; not really."

After a long silence, Tony finished his coffee, looked at his watch and said, "It's three-fifteen. Let's get going."

—*mm*—

After the court filed in and everyone took their seats, Colonel Grundig gaveled the proceedings to order. "Does the defense have any further evidence?" he asked, looking directly at Tony.

Tony pushed his chair back and slowly began to rise. Before he could say a word, however, a booming voice filled the courtroom.

"Yes, sir. Chief Master Sergeant Otis Brown reporting, sir. Testifying for the defense, sir!"

Tony and Wally glanced at each other, then looked at the doorway. It was standing open, and framed a stocky old black NCO in Air Force blues. Stripes ran up both his sleeves, and rows of medals and ribbons covered his chest.

"Buddha!" Tony whispered, as he sat back down.

Chief Master Sergeant Brown strode into the courtroom with the confidence of a man who had commanded a hundred parade grounds. He wheeled in front of the court, and snapped off a salute that would crack glass.

As Colonel Grundig casually returned the sergeant's

salute, Colonel Bolte rose and came to attention. At the opposite ends of the court's long table, Sergeants Longtree and Jackson did the same.

"Gentlemen," Colonel Bolte said icily. "It's customary to rise when a Medal of Honor recipient enters the room."

The other four officers scurried to their feet. So did the hundred or so other uniformed men in the courtroom, including the lawyers. When they were all standing, Colonel Bolte returned the salute for the court. "It's an honor to have you with us, Sergeant Brown."

"It's my honor, sir."

They all sat back down as Sergeant Brown took the witness stand.

"Well, Captain Jeffries," Colonel Grundig said. "It appears that you have one more witness."

"Yes, sir. We planned to call Sergeant Brown as our final witness." Tony glanced at Wally who didn't say a word. "Would the court reporter swear in the witness, please," Tony said as he walked around to the front of the defense table.

Ruth Olmsted raised her hand and looked at Sergeant Brown. "Do you swear to tell the truth, the whole truth, and nothing but the truth, so help you God?"

"Yes, ma'am, I do."

"Sergeant Brown," Tony asked, "would you review for the court your history of service in the military?" Tony didn't have any prepared questions, and was frantically trying to collect his thoughts.

"Be happy to, sir," the old soldier answered slowly. "I enlisted in the Army in 1931. Only job I could find back in those days. After trainin', I was assigned to an engineering battalion. Colored, of course; 'cept for the officers. When the war started, I was top sergeant. We was sent to North Africa in '42, then Sicily, after that Italy. Finally, to France after the invasion. Served under General McAuliffe in the 101st Airborne Division. We saw lots of action, sir, lots of action. Not many of the original boys was left by the time we got to France. Kept on gettin' new fellas, though."

Tony glanced at the men on the court. All except Grundig and Smithfield were leaning forward and paying close attention.

"Were you ever wounded in combat, sergeant?" Tony asked. "Did you ever earn a Purple Heart?"

"Oh yes, sir," Sergeant Brown smiled. "These are Purple Hearts, sir." He pointed to a row of ribbons on his chest. "Two in North Africa, two in Europe and one in Korea, sir. Lost this in Korea, sir." He held up his left hand with the missing middle finger.

"Sergeant, I heard Colonel Bolte mention the Congressional Medal of Honor a few moments ago. Have you received the Congressional Medal of Honor?"

"Yes, sir," the old man answered proudly.

"Where did you receive it, sergeant?"

"At Bastogne, sir. We was supposed to be engineers, but we was riflemen at Bastogne." He paused. "Everyone was a rifleman at Bastogne, sir."

"What happened, sergeant?"

Sergeant Brown looked down for a moment, shifting his weight in the wooden chair.

"When the Germans swept by," he said, looking back to Tony, "we was told to hold the road to Houffalize, on the north side of the town. Keep 'em out at all cost. Terrible fightin', sir. My boys was gonna show they was as good as the white G.I.'s. And they did, sir. Lord, they did."

The old grey-haired sergeant paused and shook his head. The room was absolutely silent, except for the faint ticking of the wall clock's second hand. Donovan rose, as though to object, then paused and sat back down.

"We was outnumbered, and after a while, there weren't no officers left," Sergeant Brown continued, his mind now on a faraway battlefield. "Fightin' with grenades and bayonets mainly. Until the grenades and both sides' ammo was all gone. Then it was strictly hand to hand, bayonet to bayonet." He stopped and quietly nodded. "But we held that road, sir. Them Germans never broke through."

"How many men were left in your battalion, sergeant, when the siege was lifted?"

Sergeant Otis Brown looked away for a moment. When his eyes returned to Tony they were moist.

"Just me, sir."

Tony had another question ready, but the words caught in his throat. He returned to the defense table and flipped through the notes on his yellow pad, trying to decide what to ask next. Finally, he turned around.

"Sergeant Brown, do you know the defendant in this case, Airman George Torrance?"

"Yes, sir. I do. That's him right there."

"Sergeant, were you at Blake's Tavern in the early morning hours of January 29th?"

"Yes, sir. I was. All night."

"Was George Torrance there that night?"

"Yes, sir. He arrived about midnight, or a little after. He was there until the bar closed 'bout five."

Tony felt a wave of relief sweep over him. He noticed that Captain Fanzone and Sergeant Longtree sat back in their chairs and were whispering to each other. They were both nodding.

"You're sure of that, sergeant?" Tony asked.

"Yes, sir, I am."

"How are you sure that was the 28th, sergeant?"

"Cause that was the night of the second killin', sir. The next night we was all talking 'bout it. And I remembered who was there the night before."

Tony walked a little closer to the old soldier.

"Sergeant Brown, you indicated that you weren't going to testify in this trial when I talked to you earlier. What caused you to change your mind?"

The sergeant lowered his head. He kept it down for a while then looked up, not at Tony, but directly at the court.

"I'm goin' out of here in a couple days," he said quietly. "Not to Guam, but to Da Nang. That's the recovery base in Nam for the 52's that get hit. Only problem is that we seem to be havin' some trouble holdin' onto Da Nang. I'm sure some of you have heard 'bout that."

Colonel Bolte and several other officers on the court nodded silently.

"I've been soldierin' long enough to know that you never know what might happen," Sergeant Brown continued. "Figured I should tell my story before I go. That's all."

"Thank you, sergeant. No further questions." Tony Jeffries walked back to the defense table. When he got there, he turned to the prosecutor.

"Your witness, Captain Donovan."

Wally McDonald started whispering to Tony as he sat down. But Tony wasn't paying attention. His eyes were on George Torrance. Torrance was smiling at Sergeant Brown.

"Right on," George whispered.

Buddha nodded and smiled.

Tom Donovan was still sitting at the prosecutor's table. He looked up at Sergeant Brown and asked, "What time did you arrive at Blake's that night, sergeant?"

"About ten o'clock, sir. That's the time I usually get there."

"And it's your recollection that Airman Torrance arrived between twelve and twelve-thirty or so?" Donovan was being careful with this witness.

"Yes, sir. It is."

"How many drinks did you have, sergeant, between

the time you arrived at Blake's and the time that George Torrance arrived?"

"Two or three, sir. And a hamburger, as I recall."

"What do you usually drink, sergeant?"

"Whiskey and water, sir."

"And you say that you left the bar about five o'clock the next morning?"

"Yes, sir. That's when it closes."

"How many more drinks did you have during that period - that is, after George Torrance arrived, and before you left?"

"'Bout three or four, I reckon, sir. Didn't keep close track."

"I'm sure." Donovan rose and walked around the table.

"Do you ever get drowsy when you're drinking all night, sergeant?" Donovan asked.

"Yes, sir. I do. I'm an old man, sir. Can't drink all night like I used to, without gettin' tired, sir." He paused and smiled. "Lots of things I can't do like I used to, sir."

A murmur of sympathetic chuckles bubbled from the crowd in the room.

"Do you think you might have dozed off for a while that night, sergeant?"

"Yes, sir. That's entirely possible. In fact, to be honest, it's probable. I sleep a little bit most nights at Blake's. Don't bother nobody. Off in the corner there."

"Was George Torrance sitting with you that night, sergeant?"

"No, sir. I don't believe he was. He usually hangs around with the fellas at the bar."

Donovan's questions were picking up in intensity now. Tony sensed that the lion had found another prey.

"Then you can't swear that George Torrance was at Blake's the entire time from when he arrived until the bar closed at five, can you sergeant?"

"No, sir, I can't. Not every minute." Sergeant Brown looked over at George Torrance. There was an apology in his eyes.

"In fact, Sergeant Brown, you can't testify that George Torrance was at Blake's at all that night, after you saw him arrive about midnight, can you?" Donovan barked his question out. The lion had pounced.

"Yes, sir. I can."

"How can you be so sure of that, sergeant?" Donovan asked derisively. "You were both drunk and asleep. You've already admitted that."

"That may be, sir, but George Torrance drove me home that night in his pickup. So, I *know* he was there when that bar closed."

Donovan stood still. He hadn't expected that. The lion had been trapped by the old hunter.

"I see," Donovan said quietly. "No further questions."

"No further questions from the defense," Tony said.

"All right!" McDonald said quietly as Sergeant Brown saluted, turned and left the room. "I think we're back in the ball game."

"Does the defense have any further witnesses?"

Colonel Grundig asked.

"No, sir. The defense rests."

Colonel Grundig looked at Tom Donovan. "Does the prosecution have any rebuttal testimony?"

"Yes, sir, we do." Donovan said as he rose. "We call as a rebuttal witness Major James Lee Davis, the Wing's Executive Officer. I'm confident that his testimony will resolve any lingering uncertainties any of you may have about the guilt of the defendant."

Chapter 16

〜〜〜

Major James Lee Davis reported to the Court, saluted, and took his place on the witness stand. He looked like he had just stepped out of the pages of a fashion magazine with his carefully combed blonde hair and custom-fitted uniform. Tony noticed the incredible shine on his black leather shoes. *How do you get shoes to shine like that?* he wondered.

Donovan remained at the prosecution's table. He had the witness sworn, and asked him to identify himself for the record. As Davis did so, he nodded to each of the officers on the Court, including the Law Officer, Mel Goldsmith. Each returned his silent greeting. Davis ignored the two NCO's.

Davis outlined his duties as the Executive Officer of the 379th Bomb Wing with a hint of his cultured eastern Virginia drawl.

"Major Davis," Donovan asked, "are you generally familiar with the details of the pending court martial charges against Airman Second Class George Torrance?"

"Yes, I believe I am," Davis answered, leaning back and crossing his leg.

"In the course of your duties as Wing Exec, have you learned any facts relating to the guilt or innocence of Airman George Torrance?" Donovan stood as he asked his question, and slowly walked around to the front of his table.

"Yes, I have." Davis replied as he casually stroked his thin blonde mustache, and looked at the Court.

Tony was surprised that Donovan had called Major Davis as a witness. *What can he know?* Tony wondered. He turned to Torrance, sitting at his right. "George, have you ever had any contact with Major Davis?" he whispered, "any at all?"

"No, man. I don't even know who the hell this guy is."

Tony turned and whispered to Wally McDonald. "I don't like the feel of this."

"I don't either."

Tony pushed back his chair and stood up. "Gentlemen," he said, "We object to Major Davis being called as a witness. An order was entered earlier excluding witnesses from being present in the trial prior to their testifying. Major Davis has been attending the trial; therefore he can't be called by the prosecution as a witness."

Colonel Goldsmith looked at the prosecutor. "What's your response to that, Captain Donovan?"

"Major Davis only attended the beginning of the

trial." Donovan answered. "It was after the trial began that he learned the facts that he is about to relate to the court. From that moment on, Major Davis was careful not to be present during any court session. He and I were fully aware of the order excluding witnesses."

"That's true," Major Smithfield said from the court's table. "I've noticed that Jimmy Davis hasn't been here the last few days."

Several other members of the court nodded their agreement.

"In that case, the defendant's objection is overruled," Goldsmith said. "Major Davis may testify."

Donovan waited for Tony to sit back down before turning to his witness.

"Now, Major Davis," the prosecutor asked. "Tell the court what facts you've learned relevant to the guilt or innocence of the defendant, Airman Torrance."

"I'll be happy to. It occurred in a discussion I had with the defense attorney, Captain Jeffries, early in the trial."

"Where did this discussion occur, Major Davis?" Donovan asked.

"Right out there in the hallway," Davis gestured toward the closed door.

"Who was present during that discussion?"

"Just Captain Jeffries and myself."

"Wait a minute!" Tony jumped to his feet. "What kind of testimony is this? If Airman Torrance made a statement, that would be one thing. But remarks that *I* make, outside of this courtroom, aren't admissible into evidence.

I object to any more questions along this line."

"Quite to the contrary," Donovan responded quickly. "Defense counsel is presumed to be speaking for the defendant at all times during the course of his representation, absent some mutual agreement to the contrary, which wasn't the case here. Whatever he says, relevant to this case, is presumed to be a statement by the defendant himself. The law is quite clear on that. In fact, we have a Memorandum of Law on this point, which you may want to consider, Colonel Goldsmith." He walked over and handed Goldsmith a stapled set of papers, then gave a set to Tony.

"That's crazy," Tony said. "How could I possibly. . ." He hesitated, trying to glance over Donovan's legal memo and articulate his objections at the same time.

"If you'll notice, Colonel Goldsmith," Donovan continued, "There is a recent decision of the Court of Military Appeals directly on point. It's cited on page one of our memo and the full text of the Opinion is included under Tab A."

"Captain Jeffries," Goldsmith interrupted as he looked over Donovan's memo. "Do you have any authorities you'd like me to consider before I rule on your objection?"

"Well, no," Tony stammered. "Not right now. But I certainly want the opportunity to look at the cases the prosecutor has cited and prepare a. . ."

"Can you cite any authorities that refute or run contrary to Captain Donovan's position?"

"No, not off-hand, but if I had some time, even a few hours to do the necessary…"

Again, Goldsmith cut him off. "With half the wing leaving in less than four days, we don't have time for legal niceties like that. The defense objection is overruled. You may proceed, Captain Donovan."

Tony sat down slowly.

"What in the hell did you say to that guy, Tony?" McDonald asked quietly. Torrance turned toward Tony; he wanted to know the answer to that question too.

"I'm not sure," Tony whispered. "It was early in the trial. Things weren't going well. I can't remember exactly what I said."

"Please proceed, Major Davis," Donovan said. "I believe you were about to tell us about your discussion with Captain Jeffries earlier in the trial."

"Yes. Captain Jeffries told me that the defendant had lied to him about virtually every aspect of the case. He said that he couldn't believe anything that Airman Torrance told him anymore."

"Objection!" Tony shouted, on his feet again.

"Denied!" Mel Goldsmith shouted back. "Go ahead, Captain Donovan."

"Major Davis, what else did Captain Jeffries say to you in the conversation?" Donovan asked.

"He said that Airman Torrance was guilty of these crimes. He said it was so obvious that he didn't see how anybody could doubt it."

The room exploded. Tony jumped to his feet,

objecting. Both Donovan and Goldsmith responded at the same time. Colonel Grundig banged his gavel again and again. Several AP's stepped to the front of the court room ready to restore order if required. The men on the court exchanged brief comments and nodded to each other. Finally, the noise subsided, with Tony standing at the defense table, shaking in anger.

"That's absolutely outrageous," he said through clenched teeth. "This is not admissible evidence." He was having difficulty controlling himself.

"Captain Jeffries may be embarrassed by his indiscretion," Donovan replied. "But his remark is clearly an admission against interest. It's the same thing as if the defendant himself admitted his guilt." He looked to Goldsmith.

"I agree," Goldsmith said. "The testimony is admissible. Sit down, gentlemen."

Tony remained standing, struggling to find the words to express his outrage.

"I said, *sit down*, Captain Jeffries," Mel Goldsmith repeated sternly.

Tony slowly complied, looking straight ahead. He was afraid to look at Torrance. Wally didn't say a word. The AP's moved back to their assigned positions.

"Does either side have any more evidence to present?" Colonel Grundig asked.

"None for the prosecution," Tom Donovan responded confidently. He began collecting the papers in front of him into an orderly pile.

Tony grappled with some questions he could ask Davis on cross, but couldn't formulate any that would have any impact; finally he looked up at Colonel Grundig and slowly shook his head. "No," he said defiantly, his teeth clenched in anger. "Nothing further for the defense."

"All right," Grundig said, looking at his watch. "It's almost four-thirty. We'll recess now, and hear closing arguments in the morning. Nine o'clock, gentlemen." He banged his gavel once as he rose.

The murmur of conversation escalated as the members of the court filed out. The two air policemen stepped up to the defense table to escort Torrance back to the stockade. As they began to take him away, he turned to Tony.

"You mother-fuckin' son-of-a-bitch," he said bitterly. "I thought you were supposed to be on my side! You really set me up, didn't you?"

<hr/>

Late that night, Tony lay in bed, his emotions churning with anger and frustration. He had spent the evening outlining his closing argument, but his mind was constantly going back to Major Davis' testimony. *How could I have been so stupid to say those things*, Tony said to himself, shaking his head. *Especially to Major Davis*.

And he couldn't forget Torrance's accusatory face when he was led away. Torrance was convinced Tony was in on the plan from the beginning. That was obvious. He was going to be found guilty of murder and probably sentenced to death, and Tony was part of the gang of white officers who were going to make that happen.

Maybe Torrance is right. Maybe I'm so inexperienced that I'm a co-conspirator without even realizing it. Maybe this is what they figured would happen, one way or another; that I'd make some rookie mistakes, which is exactly what I did.

Tony could feel Karen quietly breathing beside him in bed. His eyes were open, but the room was dark, and all he could see was the soft green glow of the clock on the night table. He squinted at it. He hadn't slept at all yet and it was almost morning!

I've got to give one hell of a closing argument. There'll be two different audiences. The first is the Court. I've got to convince them that George is innocent. The other is George. I've got to convince him that I'm really trying and not part of a conspiracy to convict him. That's essential. Tony couldn't decide which audience was more important to him.

Chapter 17

~~~~

"The Court is reconvened." Lieutenant Colonel Lucien Grundig banged his gavel once, and looked at the Prosecutor. The room quieted as the people who were still standing sat down. Again, the room was packed. The rustle of cigarette packs and the crisp scratch of struck matches signaled that the smokers were lighting up.

"Captain Donovan, may we hear your closing argument, please."

"Certainly." Donovan walked slowly to the front of the Court's long table, looked at each of the men in turn and began addressing the Court.

"Gentlemen," he said, "the central fact of this case, which defense counsel has been working hard to obscure, is that this man, right here, raped and brutally murdered two innocent young women." As he spoke, Donovan turned and pointed his finger at the defendant. Every eye in the courtroom focused on George Torrance, who shifted uncomfortably in his chair.

"The defense has tried to muddy the water as much as possible to create the illusion that uncertainty exists where, in fact, there is none. But I trust you haven't been fooled. After all is said and done, the overwhelming weight of the evidence establishes beyond any reasonable doubt that George Torrance raped and murdered both Peggy Wilton and Laurie McAllister, and should be found guilty of those crimes. There is no real doubt about that. Let's go through the evidence together and see just exactly what it shows."

Tony pulled his yellow pad toward him and began taking notes. The three reporters in the first row were already writing. Grundig lit up his pipe and leaned back. His pipe's gray smoke mingled with the haze rising from the cigarettes in the court room.

"First of all," Donovan said, "we know Peggy Wilton's killer was identified as a male Negro who was driving a Ford pickup truck with a camper. Defense counsel tried to confuse the issue when those young kids from Oscoda were on the stand, but he wasn't able to do it. There's no doubt in my mind that Brenda Wendt knows Ford pickups, and I don't think there's any doubt in yours either. Her family has owned Fords for years. She positively identified the truck driving away from the scene of the first murder as a Ford pickup with a camper in back, driven by a male Negro. Those are established facts.

"Second, there are no Negro male civilians residing in Iosco County, except here on the base. So we know that the man driving away from the Officers' Club that night was an airman stationed here at Wurtsmith. That's also an established fact.

"Third, we know from Major Pawlowski's testimony that there were only five male Negroes on Base who owned Ford pickups with campers that were in drivable condition on the night Peggy Wilton was killed. Of those five men, only one, George Torrance, was unaccounted for when Laurie McAllister was raped and murdered ten days later in the early hours of January 29th -- *Only* George Torrance. The others were all either with the Wing on its exercise or were manning the recovery facilities in Alpena. That's another established fact.

"Fourth, we know from the testimony of Dr. James Cox, the Iosco County Medical Examiner, that both Peggy Wilton and Laurie McAllister were killed by the same person, a male Negro. Dr. Cox' testimony that the killer was a Negro confirms the testimony of Brenda Wendt that the driver of the truck she and Bill Carlson saw on January 8th was a Negro. The evidence clearly establishes the fact that we're looking for a single killer and that he's a male Negro.

"Fifth, we know from Dr. Cox's testimony that the killer was left-handed. Of the five potential Negro suspects who owned Ford pickups that were in operating condition the night of January 28th and 29th, only one was left-handed. That's the defendant George Torrance. That's another fact, gentlemen. Not speculation: fact."

Donovan was walking slowly back and forth in front

of the court's table as he made his points, catching the eye of each member of the court in turn. He had their full attention. "Sixth," he continued, "we also know that the killer has Type A blood. George Torrance has Type A blood. In fact, George Torrance is the only one of the five men who owned Ford pickups who could have been at the scene of Laurie McAllister's murder and who has Type A blood. The only other man in that group with Type A blood was high over northern Canada while Laurie McAllister was being raped and slashed to death on January 29th of this year.

"Seventh, we know that Major Pawlowski found a damaged man's watch at Laurie McAllister's home. It had stopped at two-forty, the approximate time of her murder, and it was engraved on the back with the initials 'G.T.'. Those are George Torrance's initials, gentlemen. Laurie McAllister didn't have any male friends or relatives with those initials.

"Eighth, we have Brenda Wendt's positive identification of Airman Torrance as the man she saw driving away from the scene of the first murder. That's a fact, gentlemen, which the defense has totally ignored. For good reason; it's irrefutable evidence of George Torrance's guilt."

Tony felt that he was being buried by an avalanche; an avalanche of evidence that, when put together, made it seem impossible to deny or to even question George Torrance's guilt. But, somehow, he had to *make that happen.*

"Ninth," Donovan continued, the intensity in his voice rising as he ticked off piece after piece of damning evidence. "We know as a matter of fact that George Torrance is a violent man; who has a long history of using knives in his violence. His violence was so notorious that at Torrance's last base his nickname was "Slasher."

"And finally, we have the stunning admission made by the defense counsel himself, Captain Jeffries, that George Torrance is in fact guilty. Captain Jeffries has spent a great deal of time with the defendant, looking into the case, and questioning the defendant's witnesses. If, after all that, even Captain Jeffries is convinced of George Torrance's guilt, and freely admits that fact, how can he have the audacity to ask us to reach a different conclusion?

"When you consider all that evidence, I suggest that no rational man can seriously argue that George Torrance is innocent. The evidence of his guilt is overwhelming, compelling. To argue, as Captain Jeffries does, that somehow we need more evidence, that this isn't quite compelling *enough*, is to insult your intelligence."

Major Clark Smithfield turned to Captain Fanzone, sitting to his right on the court. "Damn *right*!" he said in a stage whisper.

"Now what has the defense offered to counter that overwhelming mass of evidence?" Donovan paused. "Virtually nothing. Torrance's girlfriend, Lucy Jenks, testified she was with him the night that Peggy Wilton died. She also admitted, quite candidly, that she would do anything that Torrance asked her to do. I suggest to you that she has no credibility whatsoever. You can, and should, ignore her testimony. There is no other corroborating evidence that the defendant was with Lucy Jenks that night. None! In fact, gentlemen, he was not with her. That's a total fabrication. We all know that now."

"As for the night that Laurie McAllister was killed, all the defense offered was the testimony of a well-meaning old man who said that, in the course of drinking all night, he saw Torrance once about midnight, and once again when the bar closed at about five a.m. In the meantime, George Torrance could have driven all the way to Detroit and back. He certainly would have had enough time to rape and murder Laurie McAllister, and get back to Blake's to buy the boys a round of beers before it closed.

"Don't forget, though, that the bartender at Blake's, Airman Ash, said that Torrance wasn't there at all that night. Now, I know that some of you have a lot of respect for Sergeant Otis Brown; and you should. He's had a distinguished military career. But if I had to bet on who had the clearer mind that night, with the better recollection of what actually occurred, I'd take Airman Ash over Sergeant Brown ten times out of ten. I think you would too."

"But whether George Torrance was at Blake's at all that night, which is questionable, he certainly has no alibi for the time when Laurie McAllister was killed, about two forty a.m. on January 29th. None at all."

Donovan walked over to the prosecution's table, picked up two large photographs mounted on poster board, and placed them up on a pair of easels ten feet directly in front of the Court, between the prosecution and defense tables. They were color blowups of the two mutilated victims, admitted earlier into evidence. Some of the men on the court recoiled momentarily, but they all kept their eyes on the grim photographs.

"This is how Peggy Wilton looked when her parents identified her in the County Morgue," Donovan said, pointing at one of the photos. "Note the bruises, virtually all over her body. Of course, she had been cleaned up a bit by the time this picture was taken. Even so, this photo doesn't show the damage inside Peggy, which was terrible. And you can do only so much to clean up a slashed throat.

"When you look at this picture of poor Peggy Wilton, I want you to keep two things firmly in mind. First, I want you imagine how Peggy's parents felt when they saw her like this. Probably the same way you'd feel if your daughter or sister had been savagely raped and murdered.

"The second thing I want you to keep in mind as you look at this picture is exactly what George Torrance was doing, while he tortured this young girl to death. And make no mistake about that; she was tortured to death. Look at those bruises. Look at those cuts."

Lieutenant Kopecky shot a glance at Torrance who looked away and shifted uncomfortably in his chair.

"Less than three weeks later, George Torrance did *this* to Laurie McAllister." Tom Donovan walked over to the second large photograph as he spoke. He gave the court a moment to view the graphic carnage before he continued.

"Gentlemen, what we have here is not just a killer, but a depraved beast in human form. A monster of the basest order. Someone with so little respect for life and for the simplest standards of civilized behavior, that he has forfeited any right to remain living in our society. He left the murder weapon, a hunting knife, grotesquely protruding from Laurie's vagina. Gentlemen, depraved doesn't even begin to describe the kind of person who would do that." Donovan wheeled around and again jabbed his finger at the defendant. *And that person is right here, George Torrance.*

Tony felt the air escape from his lungs and realized that he had slumped back in his chair, as had McDonald and Torrance. He quickly sat up straight, leaned forward and elbowed McDonald to do the same.

But Donovan wasn't finished. "The good citizens of Oscoda are watching us, gentlemen. They invited the Air Force here with open arms, and have been gracious hosts to Wurtsmith for many years. And now two of their daughters have been violated and murdered by someone we brought in with us. They have the right to demand justice, and to expect us to impose punishment commensurate with the crimes that have been inflicted on their community."

The crowded room was silent as Donovan paused. All seven men on the Court were leaning forward, following him closely.

"There are few crimes for which the death penalty is

appropriate, gentlemen, but this is one of them," Donovan said. "I ask you to do your duty, and to find George Torrance guilty of raping and murdering Peggy Wilton and Laurie McAllister. I also ask you to impose the only sentence appropriate for crimes of this magnitude. I ask you to impose the death penalty on Airman George Torrance."

He looked at the Court for a moment, catching the eye of each court member. He turned, walked back to his table and sat down. Once again, a murmur swept the room. One by one, the men on the court sat back in the chairs. The prosecutor had painted George Torrance's guilt in the clearest possible colors.

Damn, he's good, Tony said to himself.

Colonel Grundig banged his gavel once and looked at the defense table. "Captain Jeffries?"

Here we go, Tony thought, *let's give it everything we've got. Can't hold anything back.*

Tony stood up, took a deep breath, walked over to the easels, removed the two large photographs and laid them, face down, on Donovan's table. Then he returned to the middle of the room and faced the Court.

"Gentlemen, two terrible crimes *have* been committed," he began. "And all our hearts go out to the Wilton and McAllister families. I hope that none of us ever have to go through what those two families have suffered the past few months.

"When something like this happens, there's a tremendous urge to lash out and punish someone. *Anyone.* The act of punishing, in itself, helps cleanse the sense of horror and guilt that we all feel. But be careful of that natural reaction to lash out, gentlemen. Be careful that you're not punishing the first person who comes along who *might* be guilty, under some imagined scenario. Because if you inflict that punishment on the *wrong* person, in some misguided effort to somehow even society's score, you'll be committing a crime every bit as heinous and terrible as those committed against Peggy Wilton and Laurie McAllister, putting someone wrongfully to death."

Tony stepped back and paused. He glanced down to his right, at his yellow pad on the edge of the defense table. His block-letter outline was clearly readable.

"The prosecution," he continued, "has the clear obligation of establishing the defendant's guilt *beyond a reasonable doubt*. Let me repeat that. Before a defendant may be found guilty, the prosecution must *prove* his guilt beyond *any reasonable doubt.*

"Is there reasonable doubt in this case? You bet there is. Tons of it. When all the hype and exaggeration is stripped away from the prosecution's case, all they have is a few bits and pieces of circumstantial evidence. At best. The fact, gentlemen, is that George Torrance is innocent. There is absolutely *no* basis for finding him guilty of these crimes.

"Now, let's run through that evidence once more, objectively. When you look at the prosecution's evidence closely, you'll see that very little of it has anything to do with George Torrance."

The men on the court were leaning forward again, all except Colonel Grundig and Major Smithfield. They were both sitting back with their arms folded.

"Apparently, from the Medical Examiner's testimony, both women were *probably* killed by the same person, a male Negro. I'm willing to accept that as a possibility. I'm also willing to accept the fact that the murderer was *probably* stationed at Wurtsmith. We don't know that for sure. It might have been someone from Saginaw or even Detroit who has a hunting cabin up here or was just driving through and then drove back two weeks later. But even if we assume that the killer was a Wurtsmith Airman. Where does that get us? All that gets us is a list of *eleven hundred* possible suspects. That's how many black male airmen are assigned to this base; eleven hundred.

"It's the next step, trying to cut that list down, that gets the prosecution in trouble. Captain Donovan wants us to accept, as an act of faith, that the killer was driving a Ford pickup truck with a camper. If we buy that premise, we're led conveniently to George Torrance. But if that premise is wrong, if the killer was driving anything other than a Ford pickup, there's a whole universe of possible suspects out there who haven't been considered. And that, I suggest, is exactly what's happened here. The prosecution's fundamental premise, upon which their entire case is based, is wrong. You cannot assume that the murderer was driving a Ford pickup.

"The premise that a Ford pickup was involved," Tony continued, "is based entirely on the testimony of one person, Brenda Wendt. Remember, her boyfriend, Bill Carlson, denied being able to identify that passing truck as a Ford; his testimony along those lines was stricken. He laid that responsibility onto Brenda. Yet, when we tested Brenda, right here in this courtroom, she clearly had trouble distinguishing a Ford pickup from a Dodge. For all we know, there are other makes that would give her similar problems.

"We put into evidence the fact that there are eleven Dodge pickups with campers owned by male Negroes on this base. That's eleven more men who should have been added to Major Pawlowski's list of possible suspects. No one knows what those men were doing on the nights of both murders; or what their blood types are; or even whether they're left-handed or right-handed. But when you add George Torrance to that list of eleven, you've got a one out of twelve likelihood that Airman Torrance was the murderer. That's about eight percent, if I remember my math. Less than that, if some other make of truck was involved."

"Now, I'm not much of a gambler; some of you may be. It sounds like Captain Donovan is. But it sure doesn't seem to me that an eight percent chance of being right is a very high probability. In fact, it seems to me that twelve-to-one is a hell of a long shot. Or, to put it in the context of this trial, is there a reasonable doubt that they've arrested the right man? There sure is."

Tony turned and walked back toward the defense table. As he did, he glanced up and caught Karen's eyes.

She was sitting in the second row with Patty McDonald. She smiled at him and nodded. Behind her Tony saw the hundred other spectators, all watching him. He had forgotten they were all there. It unnerved him for a moment, and he looked down at the outline he'd left on the table collecting his thoughts.

Turning back to the court, Tony continued. "Now, the prosecution's answer to all that is to say that they have an eyewitness; Brenda Wendt actually identified George Torrance as the man driving away that first night. Nonsense! She didn't identify Airman Torrance at all, and we know that. You'll recall that she couldn't locate him in the room until Captain Donovan stood right behind the defendant. You all saw that. And then she admitted that she thinks that all Negro men look a lot alike. What kind of identification is that? It's no identification at all, and you should ignore that testimony.

"What else does the prosecution have? A phantom watch with some initials on the back? What watch? Did you see any initials? I didn't. It was conveniently lost before any of us could take a look at it.

"By the way, gentlemen, while we're talking about initials, take a look at that list of negro airmen on base who own *Dodge* pickups with campers. One of them is Gregory Traper. His initials are G.T." Tony paused and looked up and down the court. He wanted them to think about that.

"How about Eugene Toffolo?" Tony continued. "He's on that list also. Do you think his friends might call him

Gene? That would make his initials G.T. too. So even if you assume that the killer's initials are G.T., which I suggest is *not* a valid assumption, the chances that it was George Torrance are no more than one out of three."

Tony noticed Captain Fanzone and Sergeant Longtree exchanging comments and nodding. He hoped they were agreeing with him.

"Finally, in a desperate move, the prosecution says that they have some sort of an admission of Airman Torrance's guilt from me. I've got to tell you gentlemen that I've never been angrier in all my life than when I heard that. First of all, it was not an accurate quote of what I said. Secondly, since Captain Donovan has made my personal opinion an issue in this case, I can tell you that I am quite confident of George Torrance's innocence. In fact, I'm *certain* of it!" Tony paused to catch his breath.

"Where was George Torrance on those two nights?" Tony asked as he looked up and down the court. "You know where he was. He was in the barracks with his girlfriend Lucy Jenks on January 8th, and drinking with Sergeant Brown, among others, at Blake's Tavern at two a.m. on January 29th until he drove Sargent Brown home when the bar closed at five a.m. It was not easy for either of them to come in and testify here. I think you could all sense that. But they did, because it was the right thing to do."

Tony walked over to Torrance, stood beside him, and put his hand on his shoulder. "George Torrance is an innocent man. He has gone through hell in facing these charges. All because he's a Negro who had the bad luck of owning a pickup truck in Iosco County, Michigan at the wrong time. There's not a shred of credible evidence that he had anything to do with either crime. None whatsoever.

"Your responsibility, gentlemen, is to render justice. George Torrance is entitled to that justice, just as you would be if you were sitting in his chair. Do your duty; do the honorable thing; and find George Torrance *not guilty*."

Tony stepped over to his chair and sat down. He was perspiring, and his shirt was soaked. The chill of the room made him shiver. He had to hold the edge of the table with both hands to control his shaking. He sensed that George Torrance was looking at him. Tony glanced to his right. Torrance caught his eye and nodded once. He approved.

"All right, gentlemen," Colonel Grundig said, banging his gavel. "The court will retire to go into closed session. All parties will be advised when a verdict has been reached; but I would like us to render a verdict this afternoon."

Chapter 18

～*m*～

Colonel Mike Bolte was the last one to enter the small conference room that had been set aside for the court's deliberations. He was troubled by what he had heard the past week in the trial. He was also troubled by the fact that his Squadron would be leaving Wurtsmith for Guam in three days, and he desperately needed some time to deal with the host of administrative details that such a move entails. As far as he was concerned, they had to make a final decision that afternoon, either way.

He shut the door behind him, took an empty seat between Captain Fanzone and Major Smithfield, unbuttoned his uniform jacket and hung it over the back of his chair. All the others followed suit except Colonel Grundig at the head of the table. They were in a small windowless interior room and its only furniture was an eight-foot table with a Formica top surrounded by folding chairs. A pair of fluorescent ceiling lights lit the room. An old framed picture of a B-29 hung on one wall. Bolte couldn't recall what this room had ever been used for previously.

A steaming pot of coffee and a stack of paper cups were in the center of the table. Yellow pads and pencils were at every place.

"All right, gentlemen," Grundig began. "I don't think we have to spend a great deal of time on this. The man's obviously guilty. I'm sure we can agree on that. Captain Donovan did a nice job of summarizing the evidence along those lines. The only place there might be some need for discussion is the appropriate penalty for a murdering son-of-a-bitch like Torrance."

"I agree," Major Smithfield said. "As far as I'm concerned, I'm ready to vote for the death penalty. Once you accept the fact that Torrance is guilty, I don't know how you can avoid imposing the death penalty. If there's ever been a case where it's appropriate, this is the case." He lit a cigarette and tossed the match into one of the aluminum ashtrays scattered around the table.

"Wait a minute," Bolte said. "You guys are getting ahead of me. I'd like us to consider the basic question of guilt or innocence. I think the defense raised some issues that we should at least talk about."

"Mike," Grundig responded, "You're not sticking up for a bum like Torrance, are you? The guy's a disgrace to the Air Force. You're a West Point man. I'd expect you to come down hard on a scumbag like that."

"Lucien, I don't want that guy in the Air Force any more than you do," Bolte answered. "And I sure as hell don't want him touching any plane that I'm going to be flying. But am I willing to send him to his death because he's a bum? Or even convict him? No, I'm not. Jeffries made a good point in there about our honor, and our responsibilities. That's what I'm thinking about."

"Colonel, I don't see what there is to even talk about on the question of guilt or innocence," Smithfield responded. "Even his own lawyer admitted his guilt to Jimmy Davis." He turned to Grundig and laughed, "Boy, did you see the look on Jeffries' face when Jimmy Davis told us what he had said? Jeffries was dying. When he sat down he was afraid to even look at Torrance."

Grundig joined in his chuckle, turned to Bolte, and said, "What about that, Mike? Do you want to just ignore the fact that Torrance's own lawyer admitted his guilt? I don't really know Jeffries, and he seems like a decent guy, but he really blew it on that one."

Bolte reached forward and grabbed the handle on the pot of coffee. He poured himself a cup, took a sip, then looked up at Grundig.

"Lucien," he said, "if you don't mind, I'm going to take Jimmy Davis' testimony with a grain of salt. Maybe two grains. Believe me, I'm as anxious as anybody else to get out of here, but I think we should go through the evidence to see what we think is important, and what isn't. That won't take long."

Major Smithfield interrupted. "Look," he said, "Let's take a straw vote on whether Torrance is guilty of the four charges. All it takes is two-third; that's five votes. Colonel Bolte, you might be alone on this one. Let's find out."

Mike Bolte raised his hand in objection. "I have no problem with a straw vote to see where we all stand, but don't forget, it takes a unanimous vote to impose the death penalty." He turned to Colonel Grundig, "With that in mind, Lucien, go ahead and take the straw vote."

"Fine. All right, gentlemen," Grundig said, "the question is whether Airman Torrance should be found guilty of two counts of murder and two counts of aggravated rape, on the basis of the evidence that's been presented to us. We're going to go down the list in order of rank." Colonel Grundig pulled over one of the yellow pads. "I've already made it clear how I feel about it," he said as he printed the word 'Guilty' and placed a mark beside it. "The man's guilty."

"I'm not convinced yet," Mike Bolte said. "At this point, I'm inclined to vote 'not guilty'." Colonel Grundig printed "N.G." and made the appropriate mark on his pad.

"He's guilty as far as I'm concerned," Major Smithfield said.

Colonel Grundig noted this, then looked up at Captain Fanzone.

"Not guilty," Fanzone said, as he leaned over, pouring himself a cup of coffee. Grundig looked surprised. He stared at Fanzone for a moment, then made his notation. "Lieutenant Kopecky?" he said, "What's your vote?"

"I think he's guilty," Kopecky said. "He has that look in his eyes. I just don't trust him, and I don't believe his testimony. That's my gut reaction. Besides, he seems to have a history of violence."

"What kind of a vote is that, Kopecky?" Mike Bolte asked loudly, throwing his hands in the air. "You're supposed to base your decision on the evidence. . ."

"Just a minute, Mike," Lucien Grundig interrupted, raising his voice. "I'm not going to have you intimidating members of this court martial. The lieutenant voted 'guilty' in good conscience. He's entitled to his vote, and for whatever reasons he wants."

Mike Bolte lowered his hands and nodded his head. He knew he'd made a mistake in questioning Kopecky's vote. "You're right," he said quietly. "I apologize, Lieutenant. Go ahead, Lucien."

"Sergeant Jackson?"

Marcus Jackson lit a cigarette, and slowly blew out a stream of smoke. "Guilty as charged," he said, looking at Colonel Grundig.

A trace of a smile crossed Grundig's face. "Sergeant Longtree?" he asked confidently.

The sergeant waited a moment before answering. He was looking down at the table and toying with a pencil. "You know," he said finally, "George Torrance is one of the dirtiest bastards I've ever known. We were stationed together at Barksdale, and I know some things about him that none of you guys do. I wouldn't trust him if he told me it was raining in the middle of a thunderstorm. "Hell," he said with a smile as he looked up at the other six men, "I was ready to vote 'guilty' as soon as I heard the defendant's name."

Colonel Grundig raised his pencil and began to make

a mark. Longtree stopped him with a raised hand.

"But that changed," he continued, "when Otis Brown testified that Torrance was at Blake's the night of the second killing. Sergeant Brown is the most honorable man I've ever known. He's as clean as George Torrance is dirty. If Otis Brown says Torrance was at Blake's that night, then, by God, he was. Gentlemen, I vote 'not guilty'."

Mike Bolte sat back, smiling.

"Well," Grundig said, shaking his head. "We have four men voting for conviction: myself, Major Smithfield, Lieutenant Kopecky, and Sergeant Jackson. The other three votes are for acquittal; that's Colonel Bolte, Captain Fanzone and Sergeant Longtree. We need five votes for a decision."

"Five votes either way" Bolte added, "and, if we reach that point, it's got to be unanimous for the death penalty" He stood up and stretched. Sitting back down, he looked around the table and added, "All right, gentlemen, I think it's time for us to talk through all the issues raised in the trial."

"Mike, let me ask you this first," Grundig said. "Are you saying that you're opposed to the death penalty in this case, even if Torrance is guilty?"

"Not at all," Bolte responded. "Hell, I'm not opposed to the death penalty. How could I be? I fly a B-52 armed with four nuclear weapons. I'm prepared, if we go to war, to kill a hundred thousand people at a time." His comment caught everyone's attention. They all stiffened in their chairs with their eyes on Bolte. They all knew that they were there for the same reason.

"If you can convince me that Torrance is guilty" Bolte continued, "and maybe you can, I'll vote for the death penalty. I agree with Smithfield's comment a minute ago. Whoever killed those two women should burn. If it *was* Torrance, he burns."

Grundig nodded. "That's fair enough. Now, let's start with Torrance's goddamn alibis."

For the next two hours they debated and argued about the evidence and the witnesses. Colonel Grundig had all the exhibits and photographs brought into the room and spread out on the table. They read and reread the instructions on the applicable law that Colonel Goldsmith had given them. At a little before one o'clock they sent out for sandwiches and more coffee.

Two hours later, Captain Fanzone stood up, stretched, and said that perhaps it was time to take another straw vote.

"Good idea," Mike Bolte said. "We've got to reach a decision on this."

"All right, gentlemen," Colonel Grundig said, tearing the top sheet off his yellow pad. "The question is whether you're voting 'guilty' or 'not guilty' on the two charges of murder and the two charges of aggravated rape. We'll decide on the penalty after we decide that question. Is everyone ready for another vote?

Everyone nodded.

249

Tony Jeffries, Wally McDonald, George Torrance and Lucy Jenks had been waiting in Jeffries's little office since they finished the sandwiches that had been brought to them from the base Cafeteria. They had been instructed to wait there, under guard, since the Legal Office was only a five minute walk down the hall of the Headquarters Building to the room being used as the court room, and the stockade was in another building a quarter-mile away. The four of them had been making small talk all day. They were all nervous. When the call came, at three-thirty, that the Court was ready to return its verdict, they looked at each other and stood up without saying a word. The air was thick with apprehension. Tony nodded and McDonald followed him out, with Torrance and Jenks trailing close together. The two air policemen who had been outside, fell behind as they walked down the hall to the courtroom

When the court was in place, and everyone seated, Colonel Grundig picked up a piece of paper and announced that he was going to read the court's decision. The packed room fell silent.

Karen Jeffries and Patty McDonald were sitting in the third row. They had heard, like most others on the base, that the court was reconvening. The room was filled with the hundred others who had been following the trial for the past week, including reporters from the Oscoda, Saginaw, and Detroit papers. Tony noticed that Major Davis was sitting in the front row behind the prosecutor's table, along with Mitch Pawlowski.

Tony's palms were wet as he waited for Colonel Grundig to read the verdict. As he looked up and down the row of court members, Tony noticed that several of them were looking at him. *What does that mean?*

"Airman George Torrance, would you please rise." Colonel Grundig ordered.

Torrance stood slowly. Jeffries and McDonald also stood; McDonald walked around so that he'd be on Torrance's other side. Tony noticed out of the corner of his eye that the two air policemen moved in close behind them.

"After due deliberation," Colonel Grundig began, clearing his throat, "the court has reached a decision. Airman George Torrance, by the required two-thirds majority, the court finds you 'not guilty' of all charges." Grundig put down the paper he was holding, clearly upset. "Airman Torrance, you are released," he said with a subdued voice.

"Oh my God," Torrance said. He raised both hands to his face, shut his eyes, and lowered his head. Tony put his right arm around Torrance to support him. He felt George sagging into him, and Tony eased him into his chair. Tony could feel him sobbing, but couldn't hear him above the swirling noise that filled the room. Tony looked up to see Wally talking to the reporters, while a dozen other people congratulated them both. Lucy Jenks was standing in the crowd, her hands clenched in front of her, eyes shut, and tears pouring down both cheeks. Karen was fighting her way through the milling spectators; he caught her eye for a moment, and she gave him a big grin.

Tom Donovan slammed his book and papers into his briefcase. He refused to speak to any of the people who came up to ask him questions. Behind him, Tony could see that Mel Goldsmith was also clearly upset. He was sitting at his table, looking down and shaking his head.

Suddenly, George Torrance stood up, wiping his eyes. He looked at Tony and said, "Cap'n Jeffries, can I say somethin' to the court. Now that it's all over?"

"Sure, I don't see why not." Tony answered, wondering what Torrance had in mind.

George Torrance stood there, with all the noise and commotion around him, and raised his hand. *Like a kid in school*, Tony thought. After a moment, Colonel Grundig, who had been talking quietly to Major Smithfield, noticed Torrance. He banged his gavel, then banged it again. The noise subsided and everyone stopped where they stood.

"Airman Torrance," he said, "Do you want to say something?"

"Yes, sir. I do."

"Go ahead."

Torrance hesitated while looking at the men on the court. "I know," he began, "that some of you may have wondered whether I really did it or not. I know some of the evidence looked bad against me." He stopped, and appeared uncertain on what to say next. "But I want you to know that you did the right thing. I didn't do it. It *really* wasn't me. I want you to know that, now that the case is over. Thank you." He sat down slowly.

Colonel Grundig looked at Torrance for a moment, banged his gavel one last time, and scowled, "This court is adjourned." As the noise and swirling motion in the room resumed, Lieutenant Colonel Bolte and Captain Fanzone smiled and shook hands.

Wally McDonald extended his hand. "You did one hell of a job, Tony. Unbelievable."

"Thank you," Tony smiled. "You too."

Before he could say anything more, Karen threw her arms around him. "I'm so proud of you," she whispered in his ear. He hugged her back, then turned back to Wally.

"This is what the practice of law is supposed to be all about, isn't it?" he said to both of them. "Taking a tough case, with the system stacked against you, and a client who's innocent, and winning it. God, I'm floating on air."

"Let's go get a drink" Wally said. "We've got to celebrate somewhere. George, you want to come with us?"

"No, man," Torrance said with a smile as Lucy pushed through the crowd and threw her arms around him. "Lucy and I are goin' over to Blake's with some of the boys. They're buyin'! And I'm goin' there without a couple of goddamn guards! Man, I'm still in shock."

He looked at Tony, nodded, smiled and shook his hand. "Thanks, Cap'n."

Tony just nodded. Words weren't coming easily. Torrance shook McDonald's hand, turned and walked toward the door. By the time he reached it, he was surrounded by friends who were grabbing his hand and slapping his back. Others, who weren't happy with the result, simply walked past them.

"Let's all get out of here," Tony exclaimed, "while I'm still floating on air. How about the Officers Club?"

Before anyone could respond, Wally raised his hand and said, "I've got a better place in mind. Trust me, Tony."

—*mm*—

They piled into McDonald's old Plymouth, Patty next to Wally in front with Tony and Karen in the back seat. They drove out the front gate past the small group of anti-war protestors who were still there, and went north on Route 23 along the Lake Huron shoreline. The sky was a clear blue, and the late-afternoon sun was sinking into the forest line on their left.

"What a magnificent day!" Tony laughed, throwing his head back. He was sprawled in the right rear seat with his arm around Karen, savoring every sight, every color, every sound. He rolled the window partway down and a burst of cold air swept into the car.

"Hey, shut the window!" Wally shouted. "You're going to freeze us to death."

Karen pulled her coat up around her neck and snuggled under Tony's arm.

"Listen to the lake," Tony answered. "Doesn't that sound great?" The rolling thunder of the waves, only a hundred feet to their right, was much clearer with the window open. It seemed to wash over Tony and cleanse away the last doubts and horrors of the trial. But Wally was right, it was damn cold. He rolled the window back up.

North of Greenbush the road took a gentle turn to the left, then another to the right, following the shoreline. There, at the curve in the road, nestled in a stand of pines, was a little wooden building with the name "Ki Cuyler's" spelled out in bright white letters across the front; neon Budweiser signs shone in both windows.

Wally pulled off the road in front of the bar, turned around, and grinned. "Are you still a Cubs fan?" he asked.

"Is that a trick question?" Tony retorted. "Does the Pope shit in the woods?"

"That's not the way it goes," Karen said, poking Tony in the ribs.

They tumbled out of the car, pulled open the bar's wooden door, and walked in.

They had walked into a museum of Cubs memorabilia. The walls were covered with photographs and old, yellowed newspaper headlines. "Cubs Clinch Pennant!" one proclaimed. "Cubs Take Series Lead!" shouted another. These were headlines that few living Cubs fans had ever seen.

The bar was owned and run by Ki Cuyler, the son of the legendary Cubs outfielder of the 1920s and 1930s, Kiki Cuyler. The old man had gone on to Cooperstown to be enshrined that Spring in the Hall of Fame, and the family's collection of baseball nostalgia had gone on to this little saloon in the north woods. The autographed photos on the walls were of the immortals from the Chicago

Cubs' golden era. Tony was euphoric: Riggs Stephenson, Hack Wilson, Charlie Grimm. They were all there.

Wally ordered a round of beers and introduced Tony and Karen to Ki who was working behind the bar. When Cuyler learned that Tony was a serious Cubs fan, he pulled a series of dog-eared scrapbooks from behind the bar: the 1929 season, the 1930 season, the 1931 season. Tony turned the pages with a reverence usually reserved for an original Gutenberg Bible.

Wally, Karen, and Patty eased into their chairs around one of the bar's six wooden tables, laughing about Tony's fascination with the old Cubs.

"We knew he'd love this place," Tony heard Patty say. "We found it the first couple of days we were here, before we got enmeshed in the Torrance case, and thought immediately of Tony. We knew we'd have to bring him here as soon as the trial was over."

Wally took a deep draft of his beer and ordered rare steaks for all of them. He had to pry Tony away from the scrapbooks when their steaks arrived a few minutes later.

Dinner was magnificent. Tony was sure it was the best steak he had ever had. It was thick and bloody and smothered with sautéed mushrooms. The apple pie they had for dessert was equally as good, with just the right amount of cinnamon. Tony had two pieces.

"What a great spot to celebrate a great win," Tony said, looking around the table again as they finished dinner.

"Isn't it?" Wally both relieved and relaxed, leaned

back grinning at Tony. "Wow, what a trial."

"You two really didn't think you were going to win, did you?" Patty McDonald said, smiling at Tony.

"No," he answered. "No, we didn't. We realized, after a point, that George was truly innocent, but we couldn't really prove it. Not until Buddha showed up. That made it close. But I still didn't know what was going to happen." Tony shook his head and raised his glass. "Here's to Buddha," he offered. "The old soldier who won his last great battle." The others raised their glasses in a silent salute.

"Actually, Tony, I think it was your closing argument that swung it," Wally said as he put his glass down. "You were great!"

"Hear! Hear!" Karen said, and they raised their glasses in another salute. Bob Cunningham was right, Tony thought. Trying and winning a tough case is absolutely euphoric; almost as good as great sex. *Almost*. Tony couldn't remember being happier or more satisfied.

Chapter 19

—*mm*—

A week later, after much of the fog and tension of the Torrance trial had dissipated, Tony and Wally were chatting and having morning coffee in Tony's office.

Winter usually comes early to Iosco county, in mid-September and doesn't leave until late the following April. Outside the snow was still at least two feet deep everywhere. The temperature only occasionally rose to the freezing point, and the booming crash of colliding icebergs coming through the Straits of Mackinac to the north constantly filled the air. No sane man would attempt to cross the frozen water to get to the Canadian side now, but in the dead of winter, the Straits and northern Lake Huron sometimes completely freeze over and an occasional adventurer would attempt to cross the lake on foot or dog sled. A few made it, but most didn't and their bodies were rarely found.

The men were discussing where to go for a much-needed off-base weekend. Skiing, of course, was always in the picture, partly because Karen loved it and partly because there was little else to do. Tony was pushing for a trip to Caberfae, less than two hours away and with slopes, some said, that rivaled all but the best found in Colorado.

"There's an old inn at Caberfae, the Snowbound Lodge, near the slopes, that's a great place to stay," Tony said. "Very rustic, nice bar, big comfortable rooms and terrific food. I was there once in college with some fraternity guys and we loved it."

"Sounds great to me" Wally responded. "Probably need a reservation for a couple of rooms, and I'd be happy ..."

He was interrupted by Lieutenant Colonel Goldsmith, who threw open the door and stormed into the room. "You boys haven't heard about the rape in town last night yet, have you." It wasn't a question.

"Why, no," Tony said, still sitting at his desk. He glanced at Wally who silently shook his head.

"Well, Carolyn Schroeder, the Mayor's daughter was raped at the Redwood last night." Goldsmith shouted. "This guy apparently broke in the back door, found Carolyn getting ready for bed upstairs, and raped her."

"Jesus Christ!" Tony said, slowly standing.

"But Carolyn's been around," Goldsmith continued, still in a rage, "and while he was grabbing for his knife to kill her, she was able to find a knife of her own, one she always kept on her bed-stand for safety, and gave the guy a couple of chops in his side. Luckily the cook was still downstairs; he dashed upstairs when he heard the commotion. Got up there on the double, subdued the guy, who was already bleeding like a pig, and held him while Carolyn called the Sheriff.

Tony had slowly walked around his desk as Colonel Goldsmith recounted the incident; a ball of angst was building in his stomach. Wally had moved closer to Goldsmith too.

"Do they know …" Tony got the courage to ask.

"Damn right, they know. He's your goddamn client. George Torrance." Goldsmith bellowed directly at Tony. "They made a positive ID, and he's in the Tawas City Hospital right now under *heavy* guard. How do you like *that* collateral damage from your clever court martial win? And, by the way, he was wearing that same watch with the turquoise wrist band that they found at Laurie McAllister's home after she'd been killed. He lifted it from the exhibit box at the court martial, that's why it disappeared before it was formally offered into evidence."

Wally staggered back at the news and collapsed into a chair. Tony turned away, his stomach churning, then turned back to the Colonel, "How's Carolyn Schroeder doing?" he asked.

"She'll survive physically," Goldsmith bruskly replied. "But she's been through one hell of an experience that she's not going to forget for the rest of her life, that's for damn sure!"

"Does this mean that Wally and I are going to have to defend Torrance …"

Goldsmith cut him off curtly, "Hell no," he fired back.

"It seems that Mayor Schroeder has lost his confidence in the military justice system, for some reason. Since it happened off base, the case has been turned over to the civil authorities; it'll be tried by a jury in Tawas City. The two of you will not, I repeat *not,* be involved." He gave Tony a hard look to be sure he was understood, turned to Wally and did the same.

"Now I've been ordered down to the Wing Commander's", he told Tony in crisp hard words, "to explain how our office so badly fucked up Torrance's court martial. He's madder than hell and I don't blame him. We had the right man and all the evidence anyone would want to put him in front of a firing squad, but you convinced some people around here that maybe we had the wrong man; and so he walked. Now I've got to explain to the commander how the hell we let that happen. And then, you know what, *he's* got to explain it to Schroeder. The first time was easier, because maybe we *did* have the wrong man. But this time …."

Colonel Goldsmith stared at Tony, eye to eye, for several seconds, looked sternly at Wally for a moment, wheeled and walked out, slamming the door behind him.

A long silence followed. Finally, Wally quietly spoke up. "Jesus, Tony, do you realize what we did? We had a man who was guilty as hell of two rapes and murders and," he paused, "by our clever dancing and weaving we convinced the court to let him go. Damn, Tony, we told the court they had the wrong man. You swore that you *personally* knew that he was not guilty."

261

Tony grabbed the edge of his desk, slumped into his seat and stared out the window, numb. He pushed his chair back, looked down for a long moment then raised his eyes. "We were doing our job, Wally. We were assigned as George Torrance's defense counsel. We were doing what every lawyer is supposed to do, his best to win the case for his client." Even as Tony spoke, he had a rising feeling in his gut that this wasn't the way the Torrance case was supposed to end.

"Just doing our job? Bullshit!" Wally fired back "We got a serial rapist and killer off the hook when he should have been put behind bars for a long fucking time. If that's our job, Tony, I don't like it; don't like it at all! And what's the first thing he does after he gets out? Attacks another woman! I'm getting sick just thinking about what he did and what *we* did." Wally paused, shaking his head, and went on, "If, 'the right to counsel' and 'everyone's innocent until proven guilty' means what happened here, as far as I'm concerned, the whole thing is Bullshit!"

"Look, Wally …" Tony grasped for words as he looked away trying to control the anger welling up inside of him, "That's what we signed on for, as lawyers."

Tony heard an odd sound and glanced back. It was Wally vomiting into one of Tony's wastebaskets. Tony understood that too. He walked over to the window and stared out into the darkness where Carolyn Schroeder had been taken.

We were so clever, he said to himself, *we were so damn clever.*

Epilogue

"Captain Jeffries to see you, sir" a gray-haired secretary announced as Colonel Breckenridge seemed focused on a review of documents neatly stacked on the credenza behind his desk.

"Jeffries?" the Wing Commander turned and looked up briefly with a touch of surprise in his voice. "All right, send him in." He returned to the pile of paper neatly stacked behind him.

A moment later Tony strode into Breckenridge's office, gave him a perfunctory salute, which was ignored by the Colonel as he continued working on the documents.

Finally, after an awkward, long moment, Breckenridge turned, looked up and put down the paper down he was holding. "All right, Jeffries, what would you like to say?"

Keeping his eyes on the Colonel, Tony repeated the lines he had rehearsed many times over the past few weeks. "Colonel, I'd like to make a formal request that in all future court martial cases, I only be appointed the prosecutor and not defense counsel." Reaching inside his jacket he withdrew a folded single sheet of paper and laid it squarely before Breckenridge. It was the formal request he had just made. Tony took a healthy breath.

Breckenridge briefly scanned the single sheet of paper. "Interesting," he said.

"Sir?"

"Captain Donovan made the same recommendation when he left, that you only prosecute court martial cases in the future."

"Colonel, I don't want to be put in the position again where I'm appointed to defend someone, who, despite their denial, might be guilty. If I'm successful in defending someone who I believe is guilty or who I learn is guilty, I don't want to carry the weight of that decision on my shoulders the rest of my career."

Breckenridge glanced at Tony's formal request again, and looked up at Tony, "I understand son" he replied, lowering his head "and I'll put your request through today," he paused, "with my recommendation for approval."

"Thank you Colonel," Tony said almost in a whisper, as the Colonel scribbled his signature across the bottom of the form Tony had handed him, turned his pivotal chair and looked down the long run-way, admiring all the B-52's lined up, glistening under the bright crystal clear sky, and fully ready for war.

After another long pause, Tony saluted the back of the Colonel, turned and began walking toward the door.

"Oh Jeffries," the Colonel broke the silence, "as you

may hear, if you haven't heard already, I'm being re-assigned to command the Air Force Weapons Depot outside Albuquerque, effective at the end of the week. That's where the Air Force stores its worthless old relics."

"Congratulations, Colonel" Tony turned to face Breckenridge who was still staring down his row of heavy duty bombers.

"It's not a promotion, son, not a promotion at all." Breckenridge responded, still not turning away from the view along the long runway.

Tony hesitated, turned to leave and simply said, "Good bye Colonel."

"Good bye, Jeffries."

CPSIA information can be obtained
at www.ICGtesting.com
Printed in the USA
FFOW02n1249280116
20910FF

9 781478 766865